Sometimes Love is not Enough

The Evans Family, Volume 1

Robyn C Rye

Published by robyncrye, 2023.

Also by Robyn C Rye

Farnsworth Sisters
Marrying a Rogue
Rescuing Hannah

The Buckingham Sisters
Lady Maggie's Challenge
Layla's Unwanted Husband

The Evans Family
Sometimes Love is not Enough
Still the One
Moving Forward

Standalone
One More Chance
Lady Jayne's Reputation
Third Time's the Charm
Can't Stop Loving You

The Marriage Scam
An Unlikely Match
Searching For You
The Unexpected Suitor
The Lady and the Duke
Starting Over
An Unforgettable Stranger
The Duke's Revenge
The Temporary Wife
Against The Odds
Betrayed
No Good Turn Goes Unpunished
Lady Eloise's Soldier
Lillian's Forbidden Beau
Remember Me
Always Second Best
When One Door Closes
Coming Home to You
Chasing Shadows
Fool Me Once
Deserting Lady Audrey
My Unlikely Saviour
Lies and Deception
A New Beginning
Julia's Second Chance
The Hidden Enemy
The Maiden's Redemption
Miss Elizabeth's Season

Table of Contents

Copyright © 2017 by Robyn C Rye

Author's Note

Thank you for joining me in telling the story of Amanda and Scott. I hope you enjoyed their story as much as I enjoyed recounting it. I must admit that I have used the names of military training venues and installations in my narration; nonetheless, the military information in the book is based on research and my imagination. I have taken literary license, and any discrepancies in the information were used to further the storyline.

If you loved the book and have a moment to spare, I would appreciate a brief review on the page or site where you purchased the book. Your help in spreading the word is much appreciated. Reviews from readers like you make a massive difference in helping new readers find stories like ***Sometimes Love is Not Enough***.

Contact me on
robyncrye.author@gmail.com

Chapter 1

Amanda was running late. She hated being late, especially on days like today. It had been twelve long months since she had seen Todd and Scott, and now she would keep them waiting. When Todd said they were going overseas, it didn't surprise her. They had spent ages saving money for the trip, and they intended to be away for twelve months —a long time, she thought. How could she manage if they found a country they wanted to live in and didn't come home to Australia? The fear that the two men wouldn't return plagued her from the moment they left.

Amanda tucked a curly brown lock behind her ears and replayed the morning in her mind. She'd started early, but having taken the wrong turn, she needed to retrace her steps to return to the airport road. The search for a parking spot in the short-term lot took longer, so by the time Amanda arrived at the overseas arrivals, the plane had landed and travellers were heading to the luggage collection point.

Standing on tiptoes to see over the heads of the other disembarking passengers, she glimpsed a person who might prove to be Todd. The man Amanda spied on was stocky, but as everyone moved apart, she got a clear view of him. The cocky grin and quick wave told her what she needed to know. She pushed her way through the crowd and launched herself at him. He laughed as he caught her and swung her in a circle, barely avoiding an aged lady and a gentleman.

"Hi, big brother. Sorry, I'm late. I got lost."

"Hi, yourself. Is that unusual?"

Amanda looked at her brother over, and her jaw dropped. His lean body had filled out, and the tight sleeves of his T-shirt displayed his muscled, tanned arms.

"God, Todd. What did you do over there?" She grabbed his bicep and squeezed.

"We worked in a flood-ravaged district for a while. I guess the muscle results from lugging hunks of concrete from one place to another. Anyhow, let's get out of here."

As she linked her arm through Todd's, a male voice behind her grumbled, "Don't I get a welcome home?"

Amanda swung around, expecting to see Todd's weedy little best friend, and instead came face to face with a tall, muscular man with the smug grin she remembered so well. As her eyes widened, she fanned her face with her hands. The man in front of her sounded the same, but the body didn't gel with her memory.

"Ah, my welcome?"

When she stepped into his arms, Amanda felt the warmth of his body against hers. He wrapped his muscular arms around her and tucked her hair back behind her ear with gentle hands. His hard chest against her breasts caused her nipples to stiffen and her pulse to race. God, what was happening? How could she respond this way? He was Todd's best friend, and anything more would be awkward. Besides, they had shared a turbulent relationship since they were fifteen.

"If you two have finished making out, I want to collect my bags and leave. I've seen all the airports I want for the time being." A fiery red blush worked across Amanda's cheeks as she stepped back from Scott's embrace. As she walked to baggage collection flanked by the two men, she felt diminutive, even though she was of average height for a woman.

Each man left with one suitcase, insisting that travelling light was faster. But as they hauled suitcases and bags off the carousel, she realised they had lost their travel light philosophy somewhere. "How do I get that much stuff in the car?"

Watching Todd scrutinise the pile of luggage, it did not surprise Amanda to see amber eyes, so like her own, glance sideways at her. "Tell me you didn't drive that little hatchback thing?"

Amanda huffed at her brother. "No, I didn't. I drove Dad's car, but it might be a tight squeeze."

Scott laughed. "Haven't you learned you shouldn't underestimate us? We'll manage."

And manage they did. With Todd driving and Scott in the front seat, the men filled the boot and the backseat beside Amanda's position. She offered to let Scott travel in the front for more legroom, and Todd suggested he should be the driver to prevent her from getting lost again. She had little space to stretch with the front seats pushed back to accommodate the men's legs.

Seated in the backseat of her father's vehicle, which he had abandoned for a new four-wheel drive, Amanda watched the two men. Todd's hair, curly and as dark as hers, was too long, and he wore the beginnings of a five o'clock shadow. The black scuff along his jawline gave him a roguish appearance. His smile and loud laugh filled the car as he drove. Scott's cropped hair was a sandy blond colour. The beginning of a beard covered his jaw, too, and she realised they must have been travelling extensively.

"Where did you two come from today?"

Scott turned to face her; his striking blue eyes glinted at her like sapphires. An assessing stare moved from her face to her breasts and then returned to her face. Her palms sweated as he scrutinised her, and her heart caught in her throat. He gave her a lazy smile, glanced back at Todd, and then laughed. Amanda shook her head, and her eyebrow quirked at him, silently asking for an answer to her question. He slapped his knee and let out a chuckle.

"Look, Todd, she still has the eyebrow thing happening."

Todd grinned and looked at her in the rear-view mirror. He caught the momentary hurt that flicked across her face. Before he could speak, she responded; her voice was tight and low.

"Forget that I asked. I was foolish enough to think we might converse as mature adults, but I forgot you don't do conversation with me, Scott."

"Don't be angry, Squirt. We're just tired. We'll tell you later after we've eaten and slept."

Presented with his back, she scolded herself for reacting to him; they were repeating their earlier behaviour. He made it his life's mission to rile her up, and the strategy worked every time. She hated that he called her Squirt, which he was aware of. Her sister, Steph, had a warm relationship with him, but Amanda clashed with him. She had hoped that Scott might stop the baiting with their return from overseas, but this optimism appeared unfounded. The joy of having Todd and Scott home dimmed for her.

From the rear of the car, she could hear the timbre of the men's voices, but the road noise prevented their words from travelling to the seat where she sat. Unable to take part in the conversation, she gazed out the window. The four-lane freeway snaked through outer city suburbs. Many areas were undergoing major renovations as the buildings sprawled towards any available vacant land. Many old buildings faced demolition, but those with significant heritage experienced a facelift, restoring them to their former glory.

As the constructions disappeared, the road became a double-lane highway connected to the country highway leading to their home. Outside the city limits, the land that joined the streets was often barren, and at this time of the year, cattle and horses sheltered in the shade of the giant gum trees that dotted the landscape.

Amanda brought her attention back to the occupants of the front seat. They were still deep in conversation, and she wondered what they had to say to each other after twelve months together. Since boyhood, the men had been friends, and Scott became a fixture in their house after a single-vehicle accident killed his mother. With no close relatives willing to take him, he took up residence with the Evans household. Steph and Amanda treated Scott like another brother, and until an hour ago, they had never seen him as anything but a boy. She remembered the lost boy who became part of their family. The men had been friends for years and often visited each other's homes. Amanda had paid little attention to Todd's weedy little mate until after he moved into their house. At first, Scott was quiet, and while he and Todd still got up to mischief together, he paid little attention to Todd's sisters.

Somewhere around puberty, his attitude toward her changed. At first, it was just gentle teasing, and then it turned to baiting her. While he developed a warm friendship with Steph, he kept his distance from her, if possible. It hurt and confused Amanda because she idolised him like she did Todd.

Were they to return to the relationship they had before he left? She hoped for better, but her hopes were already dashed if the first remarks were a sign.

Chapter 2

Todd pulled into the driveway and turned off the car. He sighed and said, "Sis, you can't know how good it is to be home."

"I agree!" Scott said.

The unpacking of the car took a few minutes, and when they walked into the house, Todd stopped short. Amanda scrutinised him. "Wow, sis, you've excelled yourself! You've had renovations done here."

She smiled. "Thanks, Todd. I'm happy with the results. I can't think why Mum and Dad didn't have these rooms changed years ago. If you want to put your stuff in your rooms now, I can organise something to eat."

Scott picked up a bag. "Are Todd and I still sharing?"

Amanda shook her head. "No, you can have my old room. I've moved into the main bedroom."

He smirked. "You've come up in the world, have you, Squirt? What happens when your parents arrive? Will you and I have to share a room?" He leered at her.

While she understood he was joking, she couldn't stop the red blush from staining her cheeks; that would give him more ammunition against her. She shot him a glare and ignored the offer of shared accommodation,

"When our parents arrive, they will bring their home with them. Let's not forget, I own this house now and have every right to do whatever I please."

Todd intervened. "Come on, you two, knock it off. Let's put our gear away so Amanda can make us some food." After grabbing his bags, Todd headed for his room. Scott turned to glance back at her. A fleeting emotion showed in his eyes, but he walked away before she decided what it was.

Amanda sank into a chair. Her shoulders slumped, and she let out a sigh. How was she going to cope with Scott living in the house? Before he and Todd went overseas, he had been just an annoyance and a tormentor. When he hugged her, she felt a tingle of awareness run through her. Being near him made her heart flutter and her pulse race.

Todd strolled into the kitchen. "Where's the food, sis?" With his gaze drawn to Amanda, Todd saw her flushed cheeks and slumped shoulders.

"Do you want to discuss what ails you? If you take a few minutes out, we won't die of starvation."

Amanda shook her head and rose from the chair to the fridge. She pulled out a variety of ingredients and placed them on the bench. As she began peeling and cutting vegetables, Scott strolled into the kitchen.

"What's taking so long, Squirt? A man could die of starvation waiting for you to whip up something."

Todd noticed Amanda didn't answer, but her jaw clenched as if trying to stop the words from escaping her mouth.

"Ouch, I'm getting the silent treatment so soon. That must be a record; we've been home for less than an hour."

Amanda turned towards him. With her hands on her hips and her eyes flashing, she faced her tormentor.

"Scott, I hate the name Squirt, and I've told you that, yet you persist in calling me that. You are best buds with Todd and treat Steph as a much-loved sister. What did I do to warrant your scorn, abuse, and ridicule? I have spent the last ten years trying to work out why you hate me so much, but for the life of me, I can't come up with a reason. If my presence is a problem, please feel free to move out. Nobody said you had to stay after you were grown-ups, so if you move somewhere else, you won't have to see me again."

Todd watched the interaction between his sister and his best mate. Why did Scott keep prodding at her? She tried to ignore the baiting, and Todd could see that Scott's constant jibes hurt her. Something was amiss, and Todd vowed to resolve the issue.

Scott held his hands up in mock surrender. "Okay, truce. Make us something to eat, squ...Mandy, or move out of the way so I can organise the food."

Turning back to the bench, she continued with the preparations. She knew her complaint about being called a squirt was petty, but Scott's persistent tormenting and annoying behaviour was the last straw. Steph was due to arrive soon, and Amanda eagerly awaited her arrival. She would act as a buffer between Scott and herself, which should help lessen the tension between them.

As she cooked, Amanda listened to the conversation between the two men. It appeared they had plans for the future that involved both of them. After twelve months abroad, Amanda assumed there were job prospects in the wind for one or both of them, but the conversation she was overhearing suggested more travel.

The sound of the screen door banging announced Steph's arrival. She walked through the house and into the kitchen. Her brown eyes lit up, and a huge grin spread across her face as she spied the two men. Todd rose to greet her, and she stepped into his arms with a laugh. She held him tight for a few minutes, and then he eased her back from his embrace and kissed her on the forehead.

"God, Todd, it's good to have you home!"

Steph swung around and walked into Scott's tight embrace. "Ditto to you, big brother. This place is too quiet with you gone." He kissed Steph on the cheek and smiled at her comment.

With the reunions completed, Amanda suggested that they retire to the courtyard. The refurbished outdoor porch resembled a tropical oasis rather than a suburban patio. Amanda had an excellent eye for design, and while Steph had seen this renovation before, neither of the men had.

"Wow, sis, it's incredible," Todd said, looking around him.

"Squirt, the outdoor area looks great. Who did this for you?"

She closed her eyes for a moment and then looked at him. "I did the work, Butch."

Scott gave her a hard stare. "What's with the name Butch?"

"Oh, sorry, Butch, don't you approve of the name?"

He growled at her, and Todd laughed

"Well done, sis; let's see how long he takes to get the message."

Once the others sat at the outdoor table, Amanda moved inside to collect nibbles and more drinks. She heard Steph ask where they had travelled from that day, and Scott explained their recent travels. So much for a shower and sleep before imparting information on their trip, she thought. It was senseless that Scott's willingness to share information with Steph hurt her, but it annoyed her after he told her he needed sleep and a shower.

As the men nibbled their way through several bowls of food, they encountered funny and frightening stories from their time overseas.

"Tell them what happened on the train trip, Todd."

Todd let out a rueful laugh. "We had been travelling for days, and when we got to sit on the train, we fell asleep. The conductor woke us when the train reached the end of the line, and by then, we were three hundred clicks away from our destination. To make matters worse, the guy insisted we pay extra because our tickets didn't cover the distance we had travelled."

The sisters laughed. "Did you go back the next day?"

"Yeah, we did, but we stayed awake for the entire trip."

Todd's face sobered, and he shrugged. "We saw things that weren't a laughing matter. We visited places that tourists typically avoid, and we encountered areas in developing countries that were significantly impoverished. Civil wars plague so many nations, and the general population suffers."

Amanda gasped as she listened to their tales, which revealed the lack of care the men had exercised in entering war-torn areas. The outcomes from their cavalier behaviour could have been catastrophic, and she was sure that even though they made light of their experience, they must have worried at the time. Caught up in her private thoughts, Amanda missed Scott's question. She lifted her head to look at him. "Sorry, I missed that."

He shook his head.

"I thought you wanted to hear where we came from today. Am I boring you?"

"No, not bored. I'm pleased I didn't know where you two were half the time; otherwise, I'd have been a nervous wreck by the time you returned."

Todd smiled. "It sounds extreme now, but it didn't occur to us that we might be in danger. We wanted to experience the other things the countries offer apart from tourist attractions."

The two women shared a look. Scott laughed at them and pulled a face. "None of that woman's telepathy thing you two do. We've returned in one piece, and that's what matters."

The afternoon flew by at lightning speed, and as the night approached, the travellers showed signs of fatigue.

"Why don't I organise dinner, and then you two can turn in early tonight?" Amanda suggested.

Todd inclined his head in agreement, but Scott scowled.

"What? Are you suggesting that I have no staying power? I bet I can out-drink you, Squirt."

"Well, that's the difference between us. I have no ambition to be a drunk and no wish to challenge you, Butch."

The harmony of the afternoon was shattered. Amanda disappeared into the house, and Todd looked at his mate.

"Why do you do that? You know she hates that name, and it's demeaning now that she is a woman."

Steph laughed and punched Todd in the arm.

"Calm down; it's just a nickname. It's no biggie."

Todd eyed his sister for a moment. "So, is calling you Fanny fine? It's an accepted nickname for Stephanie, and it's no biggie," Todd said with a grin.

Steph's mouth dropped open, and her eyes blazed. "Don't you dare!"

"Why not? If you continue to encourage Scott, I will retaliate. I know he is my best friend, but this badgering of Amanda has gone on too long. I'd hoped the hostility would have subsided when we returned, but it hasn't. So, what's it to be, Fanny?" Todd grinned as he delivered the nickname.

Steph sighed and glared at Scott.

"No more calling her Squirt. Whenever Todd retaliates by calling me Fanny, I will punch you."

"Okay, okay! I will stop, but the problem is that I've been calling her that for so many years, I'm liable to forget."

As Steph rose to help with the food, Todd looked at his mate. "Best you work hard on that."

When the girls returned from the kitchen, laden with platters of food, they could sense the stiffness between the two best friends. Amanda attempted to reduce the tension and asked, "Are there any photos of this great journey, or were you too busy dodging danger to snap any shots?"

Todd groaned. "Scott must have a picture of every place we visited. We had some photos processed overseas, but we have just as many that still need doing."

Todd jogged off to collect the prints and returned with a large envelope and Scott's phone. After looking at the first photograph, Todd handed it to her; Amanda said, "Who took the photos?"

"We shared the duty, Squirt. I took the shots of Todd, and Todd took the shots in which I appear, as well as the shots of me. It's not rocket science; even you should be able to work that out."

She looked at him momentarily and handed the pack of photos back to Todd.

"I have work to do. I'll catch up with you later."

The others watched as she walked out of the patio and into the house. Silence descended on the occupants of the courtyard until Todd said, "Blast it, Scott! You can't help yourself, can you? Why do you do that? You two carry on, and I'll see if I can talk to her."

Todd walked through the house towards Amanda's office. He had been looking forward to coming home for the past month, since he and Scott had experienced what the world had to offer. Todd had forgotten how Scott treated his younger sister during their time away, but it had hit him full force on their return. Todd vowed to find the reason for the verbal abuse he tossed her way.

Chapter 3

Amanda sat at her desk. She realised she couldn't focus enough to do any work, but the illusion of being busy gave her credibility. Why did Scott do that? Since his arrival home, her heart pounded every time she looked at him, and her skin tingled. Seeing his transformation from a weedy teenager to a man amazed her. Something deep inside her wanted him to recognise her as a woman. How did he affect her so much and not know the tension or attraction himself? His looks may have changed, but the person inside hadn't because he still teased and bagged her whenever he opened his mouth.

How could she fix the problem that was Scott? Thinking of him made her sad; tears seeped from her eyes and trickled across her cheeks. As she rested her head on the desk, she closed her eyes and tried to compose herself. Falling apart wouldn't solve the dilemma of what to do with him. She decided to go to Myra's place and then texted him to tell him to leave. Maybe it was the coward's way out, but it was the only solution she could envisage. Staying as he took shots at her every time she opened her mouth wasn't a choice.

A knock on the door caught her attention, and she looked up to see her brother enter the room. He groaned when he saw her tears. He walked around the desk and took her by the shoulders. Amanda stood, and Todd wrapped his arms around her, holding her tight while she cried.

"Why does he do that? Why doesn't he ever pick on you or Steph?"

Todd released her and handed her the pack of tissues from the desk. "I don't know, but I intend to find out. Scott never shows a mean side unless you're around, and then he always slides in put-downs."

As the sobs subsided, she shook her head. "He has to go; I can't keep doing this. I don't want you to go, but I expect you will if I evict him. He can go to Steph's place; she finds his comments hilarious; she can have him."

"Will you wait a while for me to find out what is happening with him?"

Amanda bowed her head. "Don't take too long to work it out."

She turned off her computer and packed it into the carry bag.

"What are you doing?" Todd asked.

"I'll stay with Myra for a few days. When I get back, you should have sorted Scott out. He can move to Steph's house, which should solve the problem. I realise that if he goes, so will you, and that makes me sad, but it is what it is. Sorry."

Todd ran his hand through his hair, his mouth tense and his posture stiff.

"Don't go, 'Manda. This house is your place; you shouldn't be uncomfortable in your home. Besides, Mum and Dad are due tomorrow. They will wonder where you are if you're not here when they arrive."

She shrugged. " Honestly, Todd, I don't care. Let Wonder Boy come up with an excuse."

She threw clothes into a bag and collected her car keys from the kitchen bench. Todd let out a sigh.

"Is there something I can say to convince you to stay?"

She turned to face her brother. "I would do whatever it takes to make your homecoming happy, but I can't stay. I'll call tomorrow, and you can tell me what's happening."

Todd stood by as his younger sister walked away. He observed her as she approached her car. The small vehicle suited her slim frame, and he wondered when she had become so toned. She had tied up her wavy brown hair, and her ponytail made her look like a schoolgirl.

The drive to Myra's home took half an hour. After leaving her house, Amanda headed east towards the newly established estate. She had always looked forward to arriving home, and living alone allowed her to choose her diversions. While the boys had been away, Steph and Amanda had grown closer, but now Scott's presence had damaged that bond. Damn the man! Why did he pick on her? If Todd hadn't found the answer, her relationship with Scott would have ended. She would no longer tolerate any more insults; invitations to family functions at her house would not be forthcoming.

As she turned off the highway, Amanda wove her way along a section of road bordered by thick undergrowth. From Myra's complaints, she understood that the bushes with tiny, colourful flowers were weeds. Lantana might look great in a domestic garden, but it flourishes with abandon once it enters the scrub. The result of the growth meant that little else survived. The landholders' attempts to eradicate the weed have failed so far.

Once she left the weed-infested ground, open paddocks surrounded her. White fences separated the paddocks, and horses grazed in the lush grass, tails flicking at a persistent fly or two. Amanda saw the outbuilding that Myra used to house her livestock. From her earlier visits, she knew the building housed animals and that a tack room occupied its rear.

A cleared paddock came into view, and she braked to turn into the driveway. Pulling up at the front of the large cottage, she regretted not ringing before her arrival.

After pulling her bag from the backseat of her car, she mounted the steps to Myra's front porch. She knocked on the door and scanned the paddocks to see if Myra was out with the horses. When the door opened, Amanda fixed her gaze on her friend.

"Can I stay tonight?" she asked, bursting into tears.

Myra ushered her inside, and they settled on a sofa in the main room. "I'll put the kettle on, and then you can tell me what the problem is, and yes, you can stay over," she said as she disappeared from the room. Amanda heard her friend rummaging around for the tea-making utensils. When Myra returned, she looked at her buddy. Willow thin; she had well-defined arm and leg muscles honed by many hours of riding and working with horses. Her blond hair was held back in a ponytail, and her brown eyes and pink lips were devoid of makeup. She was a no-nonsense person, and Amanda needed her common-sense advice.

With a deep breath, she launched into her tale. Myra pulled a face at Scott's comments. At the end of the narrative, I said, "What a jerk!"

"I'm sorry I landed here without warning, but I had to leave the house. It was so exciting to have Todd back that I forgot that wherever he goes, Scott goes. My running away may be an overreaction, but I don't want to return to the way things were. If I can stay for two nights, then Todd should have moved him out of my place by then. I realise I'm a coward for running away, but having to listen to put-downs didn't appear to be a choice either."

Myra shook her head. "You can stay; that's not a problem, but fixing your troubles might take work. Doesn't your family object to the way he speaks to you?"

"No, and as much as I love her, Steph angers me. She seems to believe it's a big joke. Todd wasn't aware of the put-downs, but now he understands how hurtful the comments are. It's awkward for Todd because Scott is his best friend."

"Okay, girl, time," Myra said. "Come and help me with the horses, and then we'll eat lots of chocolate and drink wine. I've got a chick flick on DVD that we can cry and sigh as we watch."

Myra turned the horses out each morning and returned them to their stables each night. As she helped Myra catch the horses and stable them, Amanda kept busy enough to forget her problems.

Chapter 4

Todd stared as his sister drove away, gritting his teeth. This rubbish with Scott had to stop, and he needed to understand why his friend was rude to his sister. Stalking through the house, Todd stepped out onto the patio.

"Did I hear a car leave?" Steph asked.

"Yes, damn it, you did. Amanda left, and both of you are to blame."

Steph stared at Todd, eyes wide and her mouth gaping. "Me? What did I do?".

"Nothing is what you did. You let Scott get away with saying awful things to your sister while you sit there and laugh. What is wrong with you two? She is your sister, Steph; shouldn't you be looking after her?"

Steph shook her head.

"He is just teasing; he's always teased her."

Todd looked at his mate. "So, you're going to try that excuse, too? Your comments didn't amuse her; I heard her tell you to stop it. She told you to behave or leave her house. Why do you believe that what she said was a joke?"

Scott rolled his shoulders and cleared his throat. He ran a hand across the stubble on his face and shook his head.

"Ah, I knew she meant it. I've been teasing her for a long time; it's a reflex action."

"Why do you do it? Why is Amanda a target for your harassment? Sure, she's quiet, but she has a sense of humour, is kind and trustworthy, and is pretty, even if I say so myself. As my best mate, I expect you to look after my sisters, not do them harm."

"Damn, I didn't want this to happen. I had better move out; I can't have Amanda pushed out of her home because of me. Where did she go? Ring her and tell her I'll move out."

"I can't; she went to Myra's place. We've been away for a year, and she must have made friends with someone she trusts during that time. Steph, have you met Myra? Where does she live?"

Steph ran her hand through her wavy hair. The red lights in her chestnut hair shone in the waning sunlight. Her lips pursed, and she sat briefly, racking her brain.

"Sorry, I don't know."

Scott paced back and forth across the flagstone floor of the patio. "I'll go; that's the best idea."

"Not so fast, mate! I want to understand why you do this to her. It's been going on since she turned fifteen. What in the hell started it?"

Scott looked at the hands fisted in his lap. "Can we do this in private?"

Todd nodded. "I guess we can organise that. Steph, why don't you go home, and we'll be there soon?"

"Okay, I can tell when I'm not wanted. See you soon."

As Steph walked away, Scott stared at Todd. "I need a beer before I start; do you want one?"

"Yeah, why not?"

He walked back to the table with the two beers; he had a swig as he prepared to tell Todd his reason for picking on Amanda a hard time.

"Promise me you will let me finish before you pummel me to death," he said as he looked at his friend.

"Go for it."

"Before Mum died, I spent lots of time here. You had two sisters; neither one ever made it onto my radar. When I moved in here, I noticed Steph more than Amanda because of her age. I never tried to be friends with Steph, but I didn't fight it either. I thought Amanda was a pesky little sister who shadowed us at every opportunity. She was too small to keep up with us, and that's when I began to call her Squirt. I ignored her as often as possible, and since you and I did boy things away from the house, I could get away with it. Do you remember the camp we attended over the Christmas holidays?"

"Yeah, I do."

Todd didn't want to say too much; otherwise, this conversation might become a remembrance spiel.

Scott took a deep breath before he forged ahead. "When we came home from camp, I saw Amanda for the first time as a young woman. Her body had filled out, and I had a hard time talking to her. All those years of ignoring her made her wary of me, and I can't blame her. The more often she shied away from me, the more I wanted to spend time with her. God, Todd, I lusted after your little sister. I understood how wrong that was, but I couldn't stop the feeling. The only thing I could do was to make her dislike me. I've been working on it since she turned fifteen, and she might hate me, but I still want her. Now, are you satisfied?" His shoulders slumped, and he hung his head, preparing for Todd's outburst.

The low growl of Todd's laughter filled the room, and Scott's head shot up to look at his mate. "What the...?"

Todd gulped, and amidst the laughter, he said, "So, you've tormented her for years because you want her? She might have agreed if you wanted to go out with her, but I would have punched you if you wanted one of your famous one-night stands."

"I don't have relationships because the woman I want is out of bounds. You're not angry?"

Todd shook his head.

"No, although I'm unsure how you intend to fix this with Amanda. Maybe if you tell her the truth, she might forgive you."

Amanda headed for home, exhilarated and refreshed. She and Myra had spent two days talking and laughing. The break, which included feeding and watering the horses, provided her with much-needed physical activity, and the nights spent watching chick flicks and drinking wine contributed to her overall well-being.

She turned the corner and saw her parents' R.V. filling the driveway. With a shake of her head, she parked her car on the street. As she alighted from the vehicle, she saw Steph's vehicle squeezed onto the narrow strip of grass under a gum tree. So, everybody was still here. Why was that a surprise? Her mum insisted that all her children be present for at least one meal when they returned.

When she opened her bedroom door, she couldn't believe her eyes. The beautiful doona and pillowcases she purchased had disappeared. Suitcases littered the floor, and creams and lotions were scattered across the dresser top. Her confusion changed to outrage when she realised that her parents had taken possession of her bedroom.

Drawn to the noise of chuckling and chattering outside, she approached the courtyard. She slid the door open and stepped into the outside area. Her gaze skimmed the people settled at the table, and she paused when her eyes locked on the electric blue eyes she recognised so well. Scott shrugged, and Amanda glared at him, her eyes narrow and unforgiving. Glancing away from him, she greeted her parents.

"You're both looking well, Mum and Dad."

"Why shouldn't we be well?" snapped Chris

Amanda shook her head and scrutinised the couple, who were her parents. Chris Evans was thin; her black hair was streaked with grey. Her pinched face displayed a person dissatisfied with life, and she wondered fleetingly if her mother ever laughed out loud. Her dad's blond hair was now grey, and he was going bald. His perennial cardigan had seen better days, and from her viewpoint, it didn't appear that travelling suited them.

The relationship between the parents and children was never close. When Amanda left home to go to university, their parents distanced themselves by packing up and heading out into the Australian outback. Often, months would pass before news of their location arrived, and the siblings would never know how to reach their parents should something go awry. When Frank and Chris Evans decided they required a bigger R.V. for their travels, Amanda bought the house to finance their acquisition.

"Hey, sis, where did you go? You said you'd ring, but you didn't."

"Sorry, Todd. I was in a hurry and left the phone on my bed by mistake. You guys change numbers so often that I put you on speed dial so I don't have to remember them."

He inclined his head, acknowledging her reason: he had tried her phone and heard it ringing in the bedroom.

"Can I get anyone food or a drink? I need a drink," Amanda said.

"Grab a seat, Mandy. I'll get the drink for you."

Scott rose from his seat and walked towards the kitchen. Her eyes widened, and her mouth dropped open at his offer. She gazed at Todd, and he shrugged. Despite Todd's shrug, it appeared he had spoken to Scott regarding his behaviour.

When he returned with her drink, she said, "Thanks. I didn't expect to see you here."

With an exasperated sigh, her mother said, "Amanda, I don't understand why Scott was not staying here. This house is our home, and he is part of our household. Why was he staying at Steph's place and not in his home?"

Amanda sipped her drink and then placed the glass on the table. With a deep exhalation, she looked at her mother. "Scott was staying at Steph's place because this house is no longer the family home. It does not belong to you and Dad; it is my home."

Her mother gave a short laugh. "Don't be absurd, dear. Of course, it's our home."

"Mum, you and Dad sold the house to me, which means I own the house. You can't come in here, move my things out of my bedroom, and place yours there. You wanted to travel, and you have your home outside in my driveway. That's where you need to sleep, not in my bedroom. Where did you put my things?"

Chris Evans gave a huff. "Your belongings are in your room, and we intend to use our bedroom whenever we return home. Why did you move into our room when you knew we'd return occasionally?"

"Mum, you have invited Scott to return; he is sleeping in my room. Do you propose that we bunk together?"

"Don't be silly, dear! Share with Steph."

Amanda ran her hand through her hair. Strands from her tight ponytail now flowed freely around her shoulders. She sensed she was getting nowhere. She appealed to the others around the table, and her father answered.

"Amanda, we sold the house to you, believing we could return when needed or wanted to. I'm confused; what is the problem?"

"If you sold the house to anyone but me, you couldn't return. When I bought the house, I would never have taken ownership of the place if I had known you would take over every time you came home. You have your house in the driveway; what's wrong with sleeping in your bed in the R.V.?"

Scott entered the discussion by banging a spoon against his stubby. The noise drew everyone's attention.

"I will stay at Steph's for the night; that will free up the beds." After a moment's silence, the others all chimed in with their thoughts, none of which involved Scott departing.

Amanda stood. "This is ridiculous; we aren't getting anywhere. I'll be back in a minute."

Everyone at the table watched her departure in silence. After a moment's indecision, Scott said, "Excuse me," and dashed after her. Once the sound of Amanda's voice filtered through to him, he walked towards the pleasing lilt of her voice and discovered that she was on the phone. When he touched her arm, she turned towards him and glared.

"Don't leave again, Mandy; I said I'd go."

"I'm not going; I'm organising my bed for the night."

He sighed in relief but remained where he was until she finished her call. Scott's change of attitude unnerved her, and his physical closeness sent shivers up her spine. She tried to appear unmoved as she turned around to face him. The thoughtful expression on his face surprised Amanda, and she moved away from him to make the situation less tense.

"This situation with my parents looks as though it will be a long-standing problem. I never imagined buying the house could cause me grief. I may have to sell it and buy another property that is mine alone," she said.

"Yeah, this situation is tricky and will not go away quickly. Even if Todd and I leave and Steph returns home, your mother still believes she owns the house. Just don't make any rash decisions. Wait until they leave and talk to Todd and Steph before you decide." Scott looked at her, and just as he opened his mouth to speak again, Steph walked into the room. "I thought I should come and check that you two weren't killing each other."

When he threw his arm over her shoulder, she stiffened. He squeezed her arm and said to Steph,

"We're okay here, aren't we, Mandy?"

Amanda relaxed her shoulders and smiled

at Steph. "This may astound you, but Scott and I were talking; no blood involved."

"Oh, okay, I'll leave you to it then." Steph sounded peeved as she left. Scott squeezed Amanda's shoulders.

"Ready to face the interrogation?" he asked. Amanda flicked her hair over her shoulder and wiped her damp palms on her shorts. With her chin raised, she strolled out onto the patio with him.

While Scott appeared indifferent, his proximity sent Amanda's senses into overdrive. When he flung his arm over her shoulder, tingling raced along her spine. The weight of his arm and the heat from his body caused Amanda to fantasise about how things might be if he weren't touching her for show.

Chapter 5

Amanda threw the swag onto the lounge room floor as the house settled for the night. Myra had delivered it that afternoon, and Amanda decided the most sensible place for her bed was in the room the family used the least. When the house was silent, Amanda crept to the bathroom to brush her teeth and change into her pyjamas. Now that she had her sister, brother and Scott in the house, she decided buying purpose-made sleepwear instead of the skimpy boxers and singlet top she wore might be a good idea.

Amanda made it to the bathroom and back, encountering no one else along the way. As she settled into the swag, she heard a knock on the door. She sat up and faced the door. "Come in." When the door opened, Scott stood there wearing jeans that rode low on his hips and nothing else; her brain went blank. A snarling black and yellow tiger crouched on his muscled chest; its tail flicked over his tanned, firm shoulder. An extended paw, black claws bared, trailed over his well-defined abs and joined the light trail of hair that made its way beneath the button of his jeans. When his blue eyes zeroed in on Amanda, her breath came in gasps, and her pulse thumped, making her dizzy. Scott moved further into the room. "Are you okay, Mandy? You look like you might pass out."

She took two shuddering breaths and shook her head.

"Damn it, Scott! Do you have to walk around half-undressed? You've given me heart palpitations with all that buff skin showing."

He flashed her a lecherous grin and then sauntered closer. Amanda shook herself from her trance. "What do you want?"

"I wanted to talk to you, but let me point out that those skimpy little boxers and the tight singlet showcase your attributes well. A bloke could get side-tracked looking at you."

Amanda gasped and grabbed the sheet to cover herself.

"There, is that better?"

"Sweetie, I didn't say I don't appreciate the view, just that it was distracting. If you want to drop the sheet, I'll try to concentrate on our conversation."

Her eyes narrowed at him. The sheet held tightly in place, she said. "Get on with your talk, please. I want to go to sleep."

Scott sat on the chair closest to the swag and ran his hand through his short-cropped hair. "It isn't right that you should lose your room. It's unfair that you're sleeping in a swag in the lounge room. Swap places with me. I'll sleep here, and you can sleep in your old room."

Eyes wide with surprise, Amanda couldn't believe his offer. She opened her mouth to speak when he winked at her and said, "If you don't want to evict me from my bed, we could always share."

A blush bloomed on her face, and Scott watched with fascination. He wondered why she was blushing. Was it because he had embarrassed her, or was she considering his offer? "You had to spoil what was a nice gesture with an inappropriate comment, didn't you?"

"Just setting out the options, Mandy."

Her brown eyes widened, and she threw her hands in the air.

"Thanks, I'll be okay without either of your offers."

Scott stood to leave. "Mandy, it was sweet of you to let your mother off today. This house ownership thing will be a problem for you later." He grinned his killer smile at her and said, "If I behave, can I stay?"

Against her better judgment, Amanda returned his smile

"Okay, I guess so. Now, scoot, get out of my room."

Amanda stared at the closed door. Despite the time they had lived in the same house, she didn't know him at all. Amanda knew Todd had spoken to Scott about his behaviour, but the turnaround amazed her.

She would have thought this was a different man if it weren't for the suggestive comments. How was he sweet and considerate after he had made improper suggestions to her?

Amanda had discovered that she could not talk to him when he was half-dressed. How did a weedy, skinny kid, someone who had tormented her for the last ten years, change so much in twelve months? She moaned as she remembered his appearance when he came to the door, just remembering how, without his shirt, it made her flush with heat and an ache set up low in her body. Gosh, being friends with him was going to be a tough ask.

The sunlight streaming through the netting curtains woke Amanda early. She remained in bed for a while, listening to the bird sounds, but now she was awake; it was doubtful she would be able to fall back asleep. Without a clock in the room, she was unsure of the hour. The rest of the household was silent. It might be an excellent opportunity to grab a quick snack and head into her office to catch up on her work. Amanda padded through the quiet house and headed straight to the kitchen. She'd prefer to shower and change her clothes, but the shower might wake the others, and her clothes were in her old bedroom, now occupied by Scott. It was unlikely that she could hunt for her clothes without waking him.

She hummed to herself as she filled the kettle and slotted slices of bread into the toaster. She slammed into a brick wall when she turned to collect the milk from the fridge. With a gasp, she stepped back. A pair of solid arms grabbed her, preventing her from falling.

"Steady, sweetheart. You need to watch where you're going."

She slapped Scott's chest. "What are you doing in here? I got up early because the room was too light; why are you awake so early?" He grinned at her, and she ducked her head. His smile was lethal enough to seduce ten maidens simultaneously, and Amanda wasn't immune. "I couldn't resist the opportunity to see you in those pyjamas again. God damn, sweetie, you look good. You make my hands itch with wanting to touch you." As she had seen Scott half undressed the night before, Amanda knew how that felt.

The kitchen door opened, and Todd walked into the room. Amanda groaned. "So much for getting a head start with my work."

"Good morning to you, too, little sister. I'm unsure about your early start, but you should grab other clothes; those leave little to the imagination." She stamped her foot in the same way as a toddler, having a tantrum.

"Tomorrow, instead of trying to creep around, I will rummage through all the drawers in Scott's room, and I will shower, and it will be unfortunate if I wake anyone. This morning, I thought I'd grab breakfast and start work without disturbing the rest of the sleepers, but no! You two tell me that my PJs are inappropriate, and so far, I haven't had breakfast."

Todd grabbed her hand. "Relax, sis. You change, and I'll cook breakfast. We won't hold you up any longer, okay?"

Scott, who had remained quiet during Amanda's tirade, spoke. "I'm sorry, sweetheart; I didn't mean to upset you. Change your clothes, and I'll give Todd a hand."

As she left the kitchen, Todd shook his head.

"Since when did you call her sweetheart instead of Squirt? What's more interesting is how she didn't hit you for calling her that?"

Scott smiled. "I've called her that since you told me to go for it if I was serious. I'm going slow, and she doesn't seem to mind me calling her sweetheart, so that's a win for me."

Todd regarded him for a moment. "Be careful how you go. They'll watch you when the others work out what's happening." Scott gave a curt nod, and together, he and Todd began preparing the meal they had intended to cook. When the meal was ready, Amanda still hadn't presented herself in the kitchen.

"I wonder where she is?" Scott asked. "Why don't you dish up, and I'll find her?"

In the bedroom, Amanda searched through the case that her mother had stored beneath the bed. Tears of frustration welled in her eyes as it became apparent that the bag contained only underwear and socks. Where were her T-shirts and jeans? She had made a dash to the room covered with only a towel to find that most of her clothes were elsewhere. As she pulled on her knickers, the door opened. Scott stood in the entry. Amanda let out a startled cry and swung around, presenting him with her back. She heard him groan, and then he was standing close behind her. She felt his hot breath on her neck, and her body tingled. In a husky voice, he said, "Darlin', why aren't you dressed? Breakfast is ready, and I thought you were rushing to start your work."

"There aren't any clothes here, only undies. What am I supposed to wear?"

Scott rubbed his face. "Why don't you put on a bra, and you can wear one of my shirts until your mother surfaces and can tell you what she did with your clothes?" She pressed her lips together, and he watched as she pulled a lacy piece of material from the case. The creamy, smooth skin of her back, taut bottom and long, curvy legs tested his self-control. He averted his gaze with great restraint and walked to the cupboard to pull out a t-shirt. He handed the t-shirt to her. The shirt, which always looked like it had been painted on, hung on her more petite frame. The sleeves were so long that she had to roll them up. When she realised the shirt ended below her knees, she sighed with relief.

As she turned around, she said, "Thanks. Now, if I pretend there's something on underneath besides a bra and panties, I'll be okay." He pulled her towards him, and she looked up with a frown. With a grin, he said, "It's okay; I'm the only one who'll know what's underneath the shirt. It will be our little secret.

Scott gave up the fight for self-control; he slid one hand up to cup her cheek, leaned down, and kissed her. The kiss was unexpected, and she had no time to prepare for its effect on her. With her heart racing and her palms sweaty, the heat radiating from his body scorched her. As he pulled away, Amanda sighed. Taking that as an invitation, Scott kissed her again, and she wrapped her arms around his neck. With his fist anchored in her hair, he rested his free hand on the swell of her bottom and then pushed the shirt up to caress her bare back. The groan she let out brought him back to his senses. As he removed his hand, he stepped back. Amanda swayed, a confused look on her face.

"Whew! This friend thing has perks I never dreamed about." Her face clouded. "Have you done that to Steph?"

Scott smiled at her. "No, sweetheart, she's sister material; you're girlfriend material. We'd better go before Todd sends out a search party."

Chapter 6

Chris and Frank Evans announced their plan to catch up with friends after breakfast the following day. The visit provided Amanda with the ideal opportunity to discuss her predicament with Todd and Steph at the house. As Scott knew of her intentions, he poured drinks for Todd and Steph while describing her concerns.

"The problem is, regardless of how long our parents are away, they will return and expect to move back in, as though they own the house. For goodness' sake, Mum even says they own the house. What am I supposed to do? I can't evict them, yet Mum is comfortable ejecting me from my bedroom."

Todd tapped his fingers on the table, indicating he was searching for answers. Steph sipped her drink as she considered the problem her sister had inherited.

"If we show them the deeds and discuss the ownership and your rights, will they understand?" asked Steph.

Scott shook his head. "Amanda did that the other day. Okay, she didn't get the deeds to show your parents the property, but it wouldn't have made any difference even if she had. They appear to have a mental block that doesn't allow them to understand the idea of Amanda's ownership."

Todd stopped tapping and brought the conversation into focus.

"Whichever way this goes, it will get nasty, you realise? If you do nothing, sis, they'll drop by whenever they want and treat this like their own house. If you sell it, they will never forgive you."

"So, what do I do?"

"Can I suggest something?" Scott asked. "It might not be pretty, but at least you get to cover your bases. Tell your parents you can't afford to keep the house; say you're losing your job and will have to sell it. Ask them if they want to buy it from you at the same price you paid; if not, you will put it up for sale on the market. Get a market appraisal, so you know how much it's worth to list it for a real estate agent, but offer your parents the house at the price you paid."

Todd laughed and gave Scott a high five. "Well done, mate. Who would have thought you'd be that devious?"

"Okay, so we have a solution. Will you guys stay with me when I discuss the issue?" Amanda asked.

"Sure," said Steph. "You need to call an estate agent for the paperwork and evaluation. You need a solicitor, even though you used Mum and Dad's lawyer last time. You need a different solicitor this time." "

Yeah, Steph is right. Using your parents' lawyer when buying a house from them makes you wonder who the solicitor is helping: the buyer or the seller." Scott said.

Amanda collected her computer from her office to check out lawyers in the district. She chose a legal practice in the township just south of Westbourne. Amanda didn't want a solicitor who knew her parents or their history in the town. She wanted her legal representative to act only on her behalf if this became contentious.

After a few phone calls, she made an appointment to meet the solicitor and arranged for the real estate agent to arrive and assess the value of the house. Todd and Steph had agreed to get their parents out of the house, so they were unaware of the realtor's visit.

When their parents arrived home, Todd invited them to lunch the next day. The outing was quickly organised, although Frank and Chris were unhappy that Scott was not going with them. Amanda had long given up feeling miserable about her parents' fondness for him, but she knew he felt uncomfortable when they excluded her. It wasn't the right time to anger her parents by challenging their preference for Scott, but she vowed to discuss the issue before they left.

Todd and Steph had to hassle their parents the next day, as both appeared reluctant to leave. Amanda's stomach knotted with nerves, concerned that they had given themselves away. To move Chris and Frank ahead, Scott left the house and drove away as though he were going to an appointment using Amanda's car. When they realised Scott wasn't coming, Chris and Frank hopped into the car to drive to the restaurant.

Amanda heaved a sigh of relief as Steph's car turned the corner, and she lost sight of it. A few moments later, Scott appeared and parked the car in the driveway.

"I thought they would never leave. That was a good idea, you leaving. You didn't pass Steph as she went out, did you? Amanda asked.

"No, I parked in that calder sac around the corner and waited until they drove away. Now, we must wait for the real estate agent to arrive."

Scott and Amanda sat at the kitchen table. They both preferred to sit outside, but needed to stay where they could hear the front doorbell overruled their preference.

"Thanks for helping me. It isn't your problem, so I appreciate the help."

Scott was silent for a minute, and then he reached across the table and touched her face with the back of his hand.

"Sweetheart, all you have to do is ask, and if I can help, I will."

A flush covered Amanda's face, and she ducked her head. How had she spent so many years in conflict with him without seeing his sweet side? She heard him chuckle and looked up at him. He winked at her and then said,

"I'm going to make myself a coffee. Do you want one?"

Chapter 7

Once the agent left, Amanda had an exact estimate of the house's value. The assessor said the housing market had exploded, and while the price she paid her parents was the acknowledged price a year ago, it was now much higher. The estate where the house was located was prosperous and occupied by older couples who owned their own properties. The district's stability and affluence made the homes much sought after. Amanda grinned; if she sold the property on the open market, she might make a significant profit.

As they drove through the outskirts of Westbourne, en route to the solicitor's office, Scott kept up a running commentary on the people they passed and the shops and

houses. Amanda spent most of the drive laughing; she hadn't realised he was so funny. It was better to be laughing than sitting in the car, so acutely aware of him, she could smell his aftershave and feel the heat of his body.

The solicitor arrived on time and entered his office alone. Scott suggested that she see the man alone, because he might not be around the next time; she spoke with the lawyer.

"Hi, I'm Carl Bridger," he said and held out his hand. When Amanda took his hand, the calluses on his palms said there was more to this man than his immaculate suit and the air of affluence surrounding him.

"What can I do for you today?"

"Well, I'm not sure what you can do, but I have a problem you might help me solve. I need your advice, or if I'm lucky, I will need someone to do the paperwork associated with the sale of a house."

"Okay. May I record this? I'm not great at shorthand, and I don't want to miss a point that might be important in the future."

"No, that's fine." She paused while Carl fiddled with the recorder and then began again after he had identified the date and the client's name. "My parents are doing the grey nomad thing, and after the first six months, they decided they needed an R.V. instead of a caravan. They had their money tied up in the house we grew up in, as well as in stocks and bonds. The house was sitting empty for the time my parents were away, so they decided that if they sold the house, the proceeds could finance the RV they wanted."

Carl was tapping his pen on the desk, and the motion reminded her of Todd, who did the same thing when deep in thought. Amanda continued. "As it was my childhood home, I offered to buy the house, and then my parents didn't have to go through the real estate gauntlet. We had the house valued by two independent valuers and settled on the average of the two valuations for the sale price. We completed the transaction, and my parents bought their R.V. and headed off into the back blocks of Australia."

"Did you use a solicitor for the legal things?"

"Yes, we used Lewis Osbourne."

"I know Lewis. He's an older-style lawyer and suits clients of your parents' age. Who was your attorney?"

Amanda blushed and said, "As there were no difficulties with the sale, I used him. I know it was a poor choice now, but using the same person at the time seemed logical."

Carl bobbed his head. "The sale was straightforward, so I assume a problem has arisen since the purchase of the house?"

Amanda nodded and then continued. "The problem is that my parents have returned for an undisclosed time and refused to accept that I own the house. I was out when they arrived. They parked the RV in the driveway, so I couldn't use the garage. My mother packed my belongings into boxes so that she and my father could move back into the main bedroom. She refuses to allow me to sleep in the R.V., so at the moment, I'm using a swag in the lounge room."

"Have you tried talking to your parents regarding their occupancy?"

"Yes, and my mother treated it as a joke. My siblings will stay at the house for the next few weeks, but after they leave, I have to put up with Mum and Dad coming and going, treating it like it's their house."

Carl pulled out a large yellow legal pad. From where she sat, Amanda saw that her name was at the top of the page, and then he wrote dot points. She remained still while he scribbled notes. He put his pen on the desk and glanced at her. With his eyes scrutinising her, Amanda's face warmed as a blush crept up her cheeks.

Carl cleared his throat. "Hm, I assume that the house you were considering selling is the house you purchased from your parents?"

"As this issue doesn't appear to be disappearing, I might have to sell the house. I decided to offer it to my parents first, and if they can't or won't buy it, I will put it on the open market."

"And that's where you expect the trouble to arise," he said to himself. Turning off the tape, he said, "Do you have a copy of the bill of sale here and any other documents that accompanied the sale?"

Amanda pulled an envelope out of her bag. Carl flicked through the documents, a frown crossing his face.

"Damn! Lewis Osbourne included a clause granting your parents free access to the house for the rest of their lives. He has a clause on the future sale of the property. Did you read the contract before you signed it?"

Lips pressed into a thin line, she said, "Of course I did. I saw no mention of access to the house or a caveat on future sales. Mr Osbourne gave me a copy to take home and read. When I went to his office to sign, he said it was the same as the one I had at home, so I signed it."

"You've been well and truly deceived, Amanda."

She sat in her chair, eyes wide and mouth open. She swiped the hot tears from her face and said, "I guess Mr Osbourne thinks he's smart. Together, he and my parents have ruined me. Is there something I can do?"

When Carl rose from his seat, he walked over to help her from the chair. It appalled and disgusted him that parents would do this to their child, but he was even angrier at Osbourne for writing this into the contract of a naïve young woman.

"Leave it with me. I promise to do everything possible to resolve this issue. I'll call you in a few days." He patted her on the shoulder and led her to the door.

Scott rose as the door to the office opened, and Amanda shocked him when she hurled herself at him. He wrapped his arms around her and looked up at the solicitor, a question in his eyes. Carl stepped forward and introduced himself, then shook hands with Scott, who still had the sobbing woman in his arms.

"So, it's bad news?" he asked.

"Yes. Amanda will tell you at the proper time, but I will follow this through to the end," Carl said.

"It doesn't surprise me if her parents have done something dodgy. Her mother was very cocky when Amanda said that the house no longer belonged to them. Thanks for your help, mate," Scott said.

Scott wrapped his arms around her when they walked to the car. He used his thumb to wipe away a stray tear and lightly kissed her mouth.

"It will be fine, Mandy. That solicitor bloke looks fair dinkum; I don't think he'll pull any punches when he calls that scumbag Osbourne."

Chapter 8

When they arrived home, Amanda was as angry as she was upset. She updated her siblings about her parents' dishonesty. Steph and Todd were outraged and a little speechless. Neither sibling could understand how her parents could pull a stunt like that and were just as angry at Lewis Osbourne for his dishonesty.

"Mr Bridger said he would pursue this matter, but I thought some payback might make me feel better. I know I will suggest trivial things, but I aim to repay Mum and Dad. I have a few ideas; are you in or not?"

"I'm in," said Todd. Steph shook her head in assent. "Count me in, too."

"Okay. I have a few phone calls to make. After I do the first one, you guys might like to follow up." Amanda said.

Retrieving her laptop, she typed in the names of the businesses that she needed to follow through with her plan. As she dialled a number, she gave the others a grin, and then the sound of a voice on the other end caught her attention.

"Hi, my name is Amanda Evans, and I was hoping you have facilities large enough to take R.V.s."

"Sure, we have five acres at the back of the park that caters to them. When were you going to arrive?"

"I want to move the unit there this afternoon. It's in my driveway, so I need it moved soon. My parents' truck has broken down, so I thought you might know of someone who could tow it to your park?"

Armed with the towing company's phone number, she grinned at the others. "The legal document says nothing about having the van in the driveway for the entirety of the parents' stay."

Over the next hour, the sisters packed up their parents' belongings and stowed them away in the van. Scott drove to the park to pay for the first week's accommodation, and Todd chased up a locksmith to change the locks on all the doors. When the tow truck arrived to haul the van away, the girls had just completed the packing. They watched as the driver hooked it up, and they waved to him as he drove out of the driveway.

When their parents returned tomorrow, they would not be able to go into the house, and they would also have to pay for the rest of the month for the R.V. to stay at the caravan park.

When Scott returned, the girls' cars were in the driveway, and the property looked spacious after the van was removed. Although he agreed that the Evanses should pay for their deceit, he hoped that the petty revenge that Amanda had orchestrated wouldn't backfire.

The sound of the truck in the driveway announced the arrival of their parents. When she heard the key in the lock, Amanda held her breath. There was some discussion, and then someone tried the key again. Eventually, they admitted defeat, and her parents knocked on the door. Scott answered the door and let Chris and Frank Evans into the house as agreed.

"Why are the locks changed? Who did this? Where is our van? What did you do with it?" demanded Chris Evans.

Scott smiled his killer smile and shrugged. "It was a matter of necessity. Come through, and we'll tell you all about it."

"I'll just put our things in our room, and then we'll be out. The explanation had better be good," Frank Evans said.

Chris Evans stalked onto the patio, followed by her furious spouse. As Scott sat down at the table, there was a yell of outrage. "What is the meaning of this?" Chris shouted.

The siblings and Scott sat at the table, their calm demeanour denying the truth of their emotions. Amanda felt the nerves roll around in her stomach, and a lump lodged in her throat. No one spoke.

"Well? Don't all speak at once," snapped Frank.

Todd recovered himself first and took up the subject that Amanda needed to resolve.

"Why don't you sit down, and we can tell you what happened while you were away? We've been quite busy, haven't we, guys?" Glancing around, he motioned for his mother and father to sit down. With reluctance, his parents took a seat.

They devised a plan in which the boys would do most of the speaking, so that the Evanses would have no reason to complain about Amanda.

"Where do I start?" Todd mused.

"What with the whereabouts of the R.V. and the reason our belongings aren't still in our bedroom?" Frank said.

Scott spoke. "That one is easy. A council official came by and informed us that it was against council regulations to park the van in a resident's driveway. He gave us twenty-four hours to remove it; otherwise, the council would impound it. We did ask for an extension, seeing as you weren't here, but we had a tow truck move it to the caravan park. I paid for a week's rent, and if you want to stay longer, you'll need to pay at the end of the week."

"That's outrageous! Many people leave their vans in their driveways when they're not using them," said Chris Evans.

Todd said, "That they do, Mum, but as far as the council is concerned, Amanda owns the house, and you and Dad are visitors."

Chris and Frank Evans shared a look; the others held their breath. Were the parents about to spill the beans, or would they keep quiet? "That doesn't explain the removal of our belongings from our room or the keys," said Frank.

Scott took up the battle. "The girls packed up your belongings because they thought that, as you have to pay for the park, you might prefer the privacy of your personal space. The key thing is annoying. Steph left her bag in the trolley at the supermarket, and someone stole it."

With her mother and father's attention on her, Steph shrugged. "I've cancelled all the cards and ordered new ones, but I couldn't do anything about the keys. I needed to change the locks at my place, and I thought we should also change these to be safe."

"What do you have to say for yourself, Amanda?" Frank asked.

"I say we all need a drink, and then I'll think about dinner." And with that, she stood up and walked away.

In the kitchen, she couldn't suppress a smile. The execution of the plan had been faultless, and her parents had no alternative but to believe what the boys had said. As Scott walked into the room, he grinned at her. "High five, sweetheart. We did it!"

As she put her hand up to slap his, he grabbed it and pulled her towards him. "Maybe a kiss would be better than a high-five," he said against her lips. Amanda felt a tingle down her back. She ran her hands up over his chest as he pressed his mouth against hers.

An outraged cry had the couple springing apart. Chris Evans stood in the doorway, a scandalised look on her face. Her hands were on her hips, her mouth compressed into a thin line.

"What is the meaning of this? Kissing Scott like that is incestuous. How could you try to seduce your brother? You are disgusting."

Rushing from the room, Chris stalked out onto the patio area. "Did you two know that Amanda is trying to seduce her brother?"

Frank Evans jumped to his feet. "Don't be ridiculous; she wouldn't go that far," he said.

As the accusations raged, Amanda and Scott walked into the room. He had his arm around her, and Steph raised her eyebrows. Todd's face was impassive; he had warned Scott that everyone would be watching, so he wasn't surprised by the furore.

"Why don't you sit, and we can talk about this?" Todd said.

"How can you be this calm? This woman is your sister and wants to make out with your brother. What has been going on in our absence?"Frank said.

Scott removed his arm. Amanda felt bereft; his arm around her made her feel secure, and that security was now gone."Stop!" Scott shouted. A deafening silence invaded the room. The Evans parents wore similar expressions; both had gaping mouths and wide eyes. Scott ran his hands through his short-cropped hair.

"This is absurd! Let's sit down and talk about what happened."

Pulling out a chair, he gestured for Amanda to sit. He sat beside her, locking eyes with Frank and Chris. With very little grace, the other two sat down.

"Now, answer my question. What has been going on here in our absence?" Chris asked.

"Maybe we need to backtrack to deal with your first accusations," Scott said.

"If you intend to be difficult, I will throw you both out of the house," Frank said.

"Steady, Mr Ev. I will explain everything. First, we are not related and have never had a brother-sister relationship. Unless you, Mr Ev, fathered me, then Amanda and I can't be related. Next, she was not trying to seduce me; it was me who kissed her." At this revelation, Steph let out a snort of laughter that she tried to turn into a cough.

Amanda eventually spoke. "Why do you always blame me for everything? You just jumped in and assumed that I instigated what you saw."

"Of course, it was you! Scott is just being a gentleman and taking the blame for your wanton behaviour," Chris said.

"Wanton behaviour?' she gasped. "You want to see some wanton behaviour?" She turned and sat down on Scott's knee, then wrapped her arms around his neck and pressed her lips to his. He fisted one hand in her hair, and the other cupped her cheek as he deepened the kiss. The cries of outrage and disgust didn't penetrate the overwhelming feeling of desire that Scott awoke in her.

When he ended the kiss, Scott grinned. He watched Amanda's face as she refocused and stifled a moan as she licked her lips.

Todd laughed. "Maybe you two should get a room."

Remaining seated on Scott's knee, Amanda threw her arm around his shoulders, and he placed his hand on her waist, anchoring her in place. Scott looked at the couple who took him in and helped raise him. "I'm sorry if you are uncomfortable with this, but Mandy and I must do what suits us best. If you want me to leave, I will, but it won't stop me from being with Mandy."

Chris and Frank Evans left soon after Scott's declaration. The general feeling was one of relief. They were grateful that their parents believed the excuses they had given for removing the R.V. and changing the locks. The lies wouldn't have held up if Frank and Chris Evans had challenged the council about the decree to move their van.

Amanda felt no remorse for telling her parents untruths; after all, her mother had called her wanton and accused her of trying to seduce Scott. She still didn't know why she was the unloved child, and although the knowledge that her parents didn't like her much hurt, she had grown accustomed to it.

As the women packed the glasses and plates from the table, it was evident that Steph had questions she was sorting through her mind. With the dishes transferred from the patio to the dishwasher, Steph said, "Take a seat and fill me in. I feel like I've missed something, but I understand that Todd was not surprised by what happened. How did Todd know about you two, and I didn't?"

Pulling the chair up to the table, Amanda sighed.

"Easy answer first. I have no idea how Todd knew, except that he's seen me with Scott recently and recognised that the bitterness is gone. I have no idea why Scott was always such a tormenter, but I asked Todd to speak to him, and it appears to have worked."

"Sure, but that doesn't explain the kiss that shocked the parents."

"Mum walked in when he and I decided to high-five for the success of our little scam, and Scott turned it into a light kiss. The kiss on the patio was payback for Mum, but we got a little carried away."

Steph raised her eyebrows. "A little! I thought you'd start undressing each other at the rate you were going. Mum looked like she would have a coronary when Scott wrapped his fingers in your hair and kissed you senseless. At least that proved that you weren't the wicked temptress, but when did this all start?"

Amanda sat still for a few minutes, trying to put her thoughts into words so that Steph could understand.

"For me, it was when he arrived at the airport. He was always Todd's skinny mate, but when he hugged me hello at the airport, he was suddenly a man and a very sexy one at that. I don't know when it happened to him, but lately, he has become more attentive and considerate. The kiss our mother saw was the second kiss, so it's not as if this thing between us is a done deal."

A deep voice cut in.

"Believe me, Mandy; it's a done deal." Scott walked around the table and bent down to kiss her.

"You wanted to know what happened and how Todd knows, but I haven't even told Mandy.".

"Well, why don't you tell us now?" Steph said.

Scott recounted his conversation with Todd as the girls listened. When he finished his tale, Amanda swung around and punched him on the arm.

"You mean to tell me that what you have done for the last ten years was a protection mechanism for you?"

He looked sheepish. "Yeah, it was. I was sure Todd would rip my arms off if I went after you, so I had to keep you away from me somehow. What's the problem? It worked, didn't it?"

She shook her head and rolled her eyes. "God, men are stupid, aren't they?" she said to Steph.

Chapter 9

The sound of the phone pulled Amanda out of a deep sleep. The mobile resting on her bedside table rang again. She grabbed it and flipped it open.

"Good morning, Amanda," said a vaguely familiar voice. "I hope I didn't wake you."

"No, I need to get up anyhow."

"I have positive news, but I suspect it won't make for pleasant family relationships," the voice declared.

She ran a hand through her tangled, wavy hair and rubbed at her sleepy eyes.

"I'm sorry, but for this conversation to make any sense, I need to know who is speaking."

"Oh! Sorry. I was reviewing your case and presumed you'd know who it was. It's Carl Bridger. I have news about the stipulation placed on your house. I'll be in town later. Do you want me to call in and update you?"

"Sorry, Carl. The voice was familiar, but I couldn't place it. Why don't you call in, and you can meet the other members of my family?"

"Does one o'clock suit you? Your parents won't be there, will they?"

She laughed. "I don't think so; we took matters into our own hands yesterday, and they left in a huff. It might take them a while to get over what we did to them, so I'm sure we're okay with you visiting."

Later that day, when Carl arrived, Amanda introduced him to her siblings. After collecting drinks for everybody, Steph sat at the table and said, "I hope you don't mind updating us all. Even though the problem is Amanda's, we want to help if we can."

Carl glanced at her, and she held out her hand in invitation.

"Okay, Amanda told you of the condition that Lewis Osbourne hid in the contract for the house sale? It is illegal to tamper with a document, and he realised that. The agreement he gave her to read differed from the one she signed, so he committed fraud. I met with him and informed him that unless he convinced your parents to remove the clause, I would report him and take your parents to court for perpetrating this scam."

Scott whistled. "Wow, that should shake a few feathers. How soon will you find out if your threats have worked?"

Carl looked at Scott, a serious frown crossing his face.

"Soon, I hope. And believe me, mate, this isn't a threat; it's a warning and one I will follow through with if needed."

Carl gazed around the patio and said, "Nice landscaping. Your work, Amanda?" he inquired.

She smiled and said, "Yes, despite the sceptics in this room

I did it myself." Scott chuckled and blew her a kiss.

Carl cleared his throat. "Where is the R.V., and what did you do to your parents?" As the tale of the tricks and deceit that Amanda masterminded, along with her siblings and Scott, helped carry out, Carl sniggered.

"Maybe I should offer you a job at my place, and you can be the fixer."

"Thanks. I enjoy my job, but I will call you if I ever seek a career change."

The following day, there was a knock at the door. When Amanda opened the door, her parents, who were on the front porch, surprised her. "Mum, Dad, come in. We didn't expect you, so you must excuse the mess; we're having breakfast."

Frank and Chris Evans followed her into the kitchen. "Mum, do you want a cuppa?" Steph asked.

"No, thank you, we're here to say goodbye. Our solicitor has adjusted the terms of the sale, and the house is yours, Amanda. We're leaving today. I'll keep in touch."

When Chris Evans walked out of the kitchen, her children looked bemused. Frank Evans looked at his feet and cleared his throat.

"Could you take a seat? I need to explain a few things."

After a few moments, everyone settled at the table and looked at their father.

"The condition we put on the house sale was wrong, and I'm sorry. Your mother decided it was a good idea, as it could provide us with security in our old age. Lewis worried that it might all backfire, and it did when you chose a different solicitor, Amanda."

"Dad, I've always wanted to understand why Mum doesn't like me. She wouldn't have pulled that trick on the others, so why me? Her dislike of me has niggled at me my whole life, and I can't for the life of me work out why."

"Ah, that's my fault."

"How can my mother not liking me be your fault?"

Frank Evans sighed. "After we had Steph and Todd, your mum wanted no more children, but I did. When she got pregnant the third time, she was angry at me. During the pregnancy, your mum decided a third child would be okay if it were a boy. She was so sure you were a boy that she didn't pick any girls' names; she painted the nursery blue and bought clothes and blankets in blue. When you were born, it devastated her, and she was angry with me again." Frank Evans paused and looked at his children.

Amanda spoke, but her father shook his head.

"There's more. Your Mum didn't want to feed you, didn't name or nurse you. I rushed home from the hospital, painted the nursery, and gave away most of the blue things. I begged and borrowed clothes from two ladies with babies who had grown out of the newborn stage." Amanda's face flushed, her eyes shiny with unshed tears. "So, for the rest of my life, until I could afford to buy clothes, I had used clothes. During my entire childhood, I had nothing new. Mum took Steph, Todd, and even Scott shopping, and when she got home, she'd give their old clothes to me."

Frank Evans regarded his children. His face had gone a ghostly white, and a frown creased his brow. "That can't be right?"

Steph interjected. "It is true, Dad. When Todd, Scott or I had a birthday, we always had a birthday party with cake and presents. Amanda had none of that."

"No, that's wrong. I remember Amanda blowing out the candles on a cake!"

Todd shook his head. "That might be the memory you have, Dad, and you are correct. The thing is, we put our pocket money together every year to buy her a cake."

"Why did I never realise? Your mother seemed happy when Scott moved in with us; she had her second son, but it never occurred to me that you were missing out, Amanda. I'm sorry."

When Frank Evans left, his children remained at the table. "You understand, don't you, sis, that it's Mum who's at fault, not you? You were a kid, and you didn't ask to be born," Steph said.

Amanda agreed. "Dad must accept part of the blame. If he wanted another child, and Mum didn't, he should have paid more attention to what was happening."

Chapter 10

That evening, Scott suggested Amanda might enjoy a break at the coast to take her mind off her troubles. Before she could answer, Steph spoke, "What a brilliant idea! Todd and I adore the beach; we'll join you."

"Steph, I didn't invite you. I wanted Mandy to come with me."

"Don't fuss, Scott. It will be great for us to escape for a while."

The plan to have Amanda to himself had failed, and he had to share a cabin with Todd instead. As he paced backwards and forwards, he glared at his friend. "This is my best chance to be alone with Mandy. Once we tell the girls our news, they will ditch me fast. I want a few days alone before everything falls apart. Can't you talk Steph into remaining at home?"

Todd chuckled. The idea of Scott asking his sister not to go on holiday to the beach made him laugh. She found the lure of the coast irresistible and confessed the truth; he loved it himself.

With an enormous sigh, Scott hopped online to check prices and availability, then arranged their accommodation. The girls were to sleep together while he shared with Todd. After they reached the coast, Scott's disposition improved. He had visions of being alone with Amanda and hoped he could dispose of their chaperones.

Not prepared to linger, the sisters changed as soon as the men placed their suitcases in their cabins. Steph wore a daring bathing suit. The top and bottom of her bikini appeared to be composed of small scraps of material. Amanda donned a more moderate one-piece design.

Plastered with sunscreen, the ladies headed for the shallows while Todd and Scott followed at a more dignified pace. Scott secured their shade umbrella, and Todd stashed the towels; the sisters had waded into the sea by then. The men raced out to join them.

Amanda's face hurt from laughing. A water fight had erupted, and now, with aching arms and legs, everyone headed to the shallows to sit neck-deep in the shallows. Scott pulled her towards him, and she screeched as the sand rubbed her bottom. She giggled and slapped at him with her hands and then settled herself between his thighs, her head resting on his chest. The proximity of bare skin and hard male muscle weakened her knees.

While the others talked and joked, Scott slid a hand under the water. He slipped his fingers into the pants of her togs. Her small gasp was the only sign that what he was doing wasn't G-rated and suitable for a family beach. She squirmed and then murmured, "Stop." He sighed and removed his hand. She leaned back against his shoulder and whispered,

"Later."

Hunger pushed the others out of the water, but Scott pulled Amanda towards him again and said, "I need a moment to compose myself." She giggled.

"Baggage!" he chuckled as she grinned and followed her brother and sister to their shade shelter.

When Scott joined them, they decided that a shower and a restaurant, in that order, were what they needed. As they walked to their chosen eatery, Scott linked his fingers through Amanda's as he chatted with others. Amanda couldn't believe she wasn't dreaming. She'd battled him for so long that now being girlfriend material made her both exhilarated and confused. Sensitive to her confusion, he squeezed her fingers. "Okay?" he asked. She tilted her head up, and the luminous glow of her eyes and wide smile gave him the answer to his question.

That night, as Amanda lay in bed, she mourned the lost opportunity for Scott and her to spend time alone. They had only managed a goodnight kiss, and every time she and Scott got close, Steph interrupted them.

"This thing with Scott, are you sure you realise what you're doing?" Steph asked,

Amanda sat up in bed, peering through the darkness at her sister. "What do you mean?"

"Well, he's a player. He never stays long with one woman, and if this goes wrong, it might ruin the family harmony."

Amanda laughed. "You only think we have unity because you're not the excluded person. I'm the unloved, unwanted intrusion in our household. If I'm ostracised because we fall out, it will not differ from how our parents treat me now."

"I guess so. Just be careful for your own sake," Steph advised.

"If you gave us privacy, we might work out where we're going with this romance. Every time Scott gets near me, you throw in interference. He told me he wanted to be with me three weeks ago, and we've only managed a few kisses because you insist on being a chaperone. These few days away should have been just him and me, and you understood that when you invited yourself and Todd. I understand you disapprove, but for goodness' sake, Steph, mind your own business."

"Okay, sis, but it's your funeral."

The days at the beach had given everyone space from their parents' problem, but Amanda's nerves made her jittery, and Scott showed signs of acute frustration. Amanda tried to think of how she could manoeuvre alone time with Scott, but before she could, the phone rang. Myra had organised a girls' night out with a few friends and wanted her to come.

"Come, Amanda. It will be lots of fun. I'm not sure where we're going, but you don't care where we go, do you?"

"No, I have no preference. Thanks, I'd love to go."

Amanda strolled back out onto the patio. "Guess what? Myra is organising a girls' night out, and she has invited me. It's been ages since I chatted with the others; you don't mind if I go?" she said, looking at Scott.

"No, that's fine. Todd and I can have a few beers with the guys.; play pool or catch up with our mates."

" Can I come with you guys? I don't fancy a girls' night out with people I haven't met before," Steph said.

They made the arrangements, and the girls holed up in the bathrooms to prepare. When Scott heard the knock on the door, he walked through the house to answer it. His idea of dressing up consisted of jeans with no holes and a collared shirt. As his hair had grown, he ran a brush over it. When he opened the front door, he assumed that the girl standing there was Myra. "Hi, I'm Scott. I guess you're here for Mandy. I'll call her for you."

As Amanda walked towards him, he let out a soft growl. She wore a blue dress that hugged her breasts and hips, then tapered just above her knees. She wore killer heels and, with subtle makeup, looked stunning. The idea of her at the pub where anyone could chat her up made him grit his teeth. When she gave him a big smile and licked her lips, his pulse raced, and his jeans became tighter. Amanda gave him a peck on the cheek, and she strolled out the door to meet Myra.

The car parked at the front of her house had only one seat left. Another vehicle parked behind the first one, and she shot a querying glance at Myra.

"We couldn't fit everyone in one car." The women decided to go to the Stockyard, a pub with music and a dance floor. After its renovation, the hotel no longer attracted the severe drinkers or rough patrons.

The drive took longer than expected as they made a detour to pick up Lola. Amanda was pleased that the woman was travelling in the other vehicle, as she found her brash. Why did Myra count her as a friend? Amanda didn't understand but would put up with the woman for Myra's sake. The ladies headed to the bar to collect drinks. A table was reserved for them, which wasn't a surprise; Myra was well-organised. As Amanda turned to leave, her glass held in one hand, she glanced up and saw Steph. She smiled at her surprised sister and followed the others in her group to their table. After good-natured teasing, Amanda chose the end seat that nobody else wanted. The position on the table didn't matter to her; she wasn't here to attract attention or flirt with strangers. The camaraderie of the ladies drew her to the night out, so where she sat was unimportant.

Steph, Todd, and Scott had just arrived when Steph caught sight of her sister. Her eyes widened in surprise when she realised her sister and her friends had chosen this pub for their girls' night out. It hadn't occurred to Steph that Amanda's friends would come to this hotel. But when she thought about it, she realised that the live music and the dance floor would be a drawcard.

Once the surprise of seeing Amanda had sunk in, fear gripped Steph. Scott was somewhere here. If she knew him as well as she thought, he was on the prowl for a willing woman; he needed to know Amanda and her friends had arrived. Steph scanned the crowd but couldn't find Scott, but Todd's head was visible among the group at the bar. Steph wove through the other patrons and grabbed his arm.

"Todd, have you seen Scott?"

Todd scanned the surrounding area. "I'm not sure where he is. Why? What's the problem?"

Steph groaned. "The problem is that he is looking for some action, and he needs to be aware that Amanda and her friends are here."

"Damn! I'll try to find him. Keep watch, and if you catch up with him, text me, okay?"

As Todd moved away, Steph glanced at the table where the group, which included her sister, sat. If Todd couldn't find Scott, the hurt she had warned Amanda about would come to pass.

The conversation flowed, and Lola made loud comments about sexy guys. The woman was a total embarrassment. Amanda felt thankful she sat at the end of the table, sheltered from the view of anyone who might recognise her. Lola disappeared for a few minutes and then reappeared on the dance floor. Amanda had an unimpeded view of the dancers, and while not much interested in Lola's antics, she gazed out at the couples gyrating to the music. Lola crawled all over the man she danced with, and they danced in a way that embarrassed her.

"God, Myra, get a load of that! Lola has no shame; why did you bring her?"

"I sometimes ask myself that. Note to self: leave Lola at home next time."

Despite her embarrassment, her eyes continued to return to the dancers. Lola and her partner were almost having sex on the dance floor, rubbing against each other, and the man's large hand caressed her bum. As the couple twirled, the man's face came into view. Amanda gasped. She felt as though someone had punched her in the chest. The pain was excruciating; she doubled over in her seat. Her stomach heaved, and tears welled as she recognised the man. Scott continued to dance with his partner, oblivious that the woman he had designated as girlfriend material had a ringside view. She kept her head bowed to block out the view of Scott and Lola, only to have her head shoot up again at Lola's voice.

"Ladies, I have met the hottest man ever. I'm leaving with him so that I can talk to you tomorrow. He looks like he could go all night, and I intend to put him to the test."

Lola giggled and said, "I'll give you a play-by-play tomorrow."

The deep male voice Amanda knew so well said, "Are you ready to leave, babe?" Lola simpered as Scott grasped her arm. Amanda stood, her face pale and tears welling in her eyes.

"I'm ready to go, too. I feel sick."

Scott's head shot up. "Shit." His face paled, and he stepped forward and reached an arm towards her. She sidestepped him and bolted for the door. Myra stood, and with clenched fists, she glared at him.

"Scott, you are such a worthless bastard. I've picked up the pieces once, and then you crush her again. It's a pity you can't keep your fly zipped, but don't let us stop you. After your dance performance, I'm surprised you have the energy for more. Take Lola with you and get out. I'm sure she can make you forget. Oh, hold on! She made you forget you have a girlfriend already."

Todd and Steph heard the commotion and moved towards the table. Scott stood immobile while a woman tore strips off him. Todd guessed that the woman must be Myra. From the expression on his friend's face, they had caught him with his newest conquest. Todd's concern now was for Amanda; to hell with Scott. "Where is she?" he asked Myra.

Myra sized up Todd and then dipped her head. "She's gone, and seeing as she came with me, that's a worry."

Todd ran his fingers through his hair. "Thanks, you continue with your night, and we'll go home."

Myra shook her head. "I can't speak for the other ladies, but I don't have any inclination to continue with the evening. Your mate and our former friend messed up our girls' night. We'll take a rain check on the night. Are you Todd? Let me give you my mobile in case you need help. Ring me when you find her."

Todd gave Myra a grim smile as he took her phone from her. Once he had entered his contact details, he scrolled through his contacts on his mobile and added hers.

As they headed for the door, Todd noticed Scott was leaving with him and Steph. He scowled at him.

"What, you don't want the hot tart after all?"

Scott ran his hands through his short hair. "God, I thought it was a good way to relieve an itch, but it has become a nightmare. No, I don't want the other chick."

Steph said, "I told her to avoid you. You've always been a player, and I said she would get hurt. Now we must pick up the pieces, and the family will never be the same with you two at odds."

Todd glared at her, anger vibrating in his voice as he replied. "Stop! Currently, we need to determine how she left. The recriminations can come later."

Todd questioned the security man. "Mate, do you remember a lady who shot out of here a few minutes ago?"

"A chick rushed out here, bawling her eyes out. She looked incapable of looking after herself, so I sent her home in a taxi."

Now they were sure Amanda had transport home; Steph and Todd had a choice: did they go home or wait and approach her in the morning?

"We need to sort this out now, not in the morning. I stuffed up, but I still need to talk to Mandy. We should go over to her house now," Scott said.

Steph shook her head, her expression one of disbelief. "Scott, I can guarantee that if you go to her house now, she will stab you with the nearest sharp object. It would be best if you waited until morning, and we must wait until morning as well. Let's give her this time alone and check on her in the morning."

Todd couldn't decide what to do and eventually agreed with Steph; they would leave Amanda tonight and visit her in the morning.

Chapter 11

Amanda was desolate. She wept and sobbed the entire ride home, and the taxi driver didn't talk after asking for her location. She tried to block out the images of Scott and Lola that kept running through her head. When the driver pulled up outside the house, Amanda glanced at the meter and, with fumbling fingers, pulled out forty dollars.

"That'll be fifty dollars, thanks."

As she paused for a minute, she wondered whether, in her distraught state, she had misread the meter. She glanced over the driver's shoulder, and the meter showed the total was thirty-four dollars and sixty cents.

"The meter says thirty-four dollars." Amanda flicked two twenties at him and opened the car door. As she stepped out, the taxi driver shot out of his door and seized her arm.

"I listened to you snivel the entire way; the least you can do is compensate me for that."

She attempted to shrug the driver off, but he hung on to her arm. "Let me go. Forty dollars gives you a six-dollar tip."

"Maybe you can repay me some other way." The driver leered at her and shoved her, intending to push her back into the car. Amanda knew that if the man shoved her back into the taxi, he could whisk her away from her home, and he could do so as he pleased. She hung onto the door frame, and her anger turned to fear when she realised the driver wasn't backing down. Would anyone come to her aid in this quiet neighbourhood if she screamed?

She opened her mouth wide and shrieked. She yelled for help and screamed blue murder. The driver's face turned purple; his rage was palpable. Lights in the nearby houses flicked on. "What's going on here?" a male voice called out.

"Mr Hoffman, help me, please."

As he raced down the house steps, her neighbour shouted,

"Is that you, Amanda?"

The driver pushed her away and slammed the back door, hitting her with the edge of the door. Amanda cried out as the sharp edge dug into her stomach, the pain as severe as a stab with a knife. There was a commotion at the front of the car as Mr Hoffman and two other men dragged the struggling driver from his vehicle.

A few minutes later, a police car, summoned by Mrs Hoffman, cruised to a halt near the taxi. Two officers exited the vehicle and moved to the area where Mr Hoffman and his friends held the restrained driver. "What's happened?" asked the older of the two officers. While Mr Hoffman explained what he knew of the incident, the second officer pulled Amanda aside to ask her questions. She gingerly moved as she tried to explain what the driver did. Once he and the other officer had the details of the incident, they cuffed the taxi driver and deposited him in the police vehicle.

The rotating strobes of the police car gave the street an eerie appearance, masking the ambulance's approach. The slamming of car doors alerted Amanda to the ambulance's arrival.

"Are you injured?" asked the medic. She shrugged. "A bit. He attempted to slam the door shut; the sharp edge caught me in the stomach. It hurts."

Tears welled in her eyes; this was a lousy night—first her faithless boyfriend and then the taxi driver. Do I have the word victim printed on my forehead? She wondered.

"If that hurts now, wait until that bruise comes out tomorrow. Not only will it look unappealing, but it will also cause considerable pain. I can give you a couple of painkillers, or you can use off-the-shelf products if you have something in the house," said the ambulance officer.

Once the ambulance driver finished dispensing painkillers and the police car cruised away, Mr and Mrs Hoffman escorted her to her home.

"Can I make you a cuppa?" asked Mrs Hoffman.

"Thanks, Mrs Hoffman, but I might have a bath and go to bed. You've been kind, coming to my aid, but I'll call it a night."

"Do you mind if I check on you tomorrow?" asked Mrs Hoffman.

"No, that's fine."

As the door closed behind her, Amanda let out a shuddering breath. A headache throbbed in her temples, and the injury on her side stabbed her at every movement. She shelved the thought of bathing; she was too tired to bother. Expecting the others to arrive soon, she locked the door and put a thong under the bottom hinge to act as a wedge. She wanted no platitudes or weak excuses from Scott. The dance floor sex was atrocious enough, but imagining Scott and Lola naked together made her nauseous. Steph had warned her to be cautious about getting involved with Scott, but Amanda was convinced his attentions were genuine. She was a fool; she should have listened to her sister and run away when he was pleasant.

Chapter 12

When Amanda woke in the morning, the house was quiet. She didn't think anybody had come home last night. Either the painkillers had been very useful, or the others had stayed at Steph's house for the evening. As she walked to the kitchen, she peered out the front window. There was no sign of Steph's car in the driveway. They must have stayed at Steph's place last night, but she could expect a visit from Todd sometime today. Steph would come too to remind her sister of her warning. Amanda realised that Steph's prediction had been correct in her heart of hearts, but she didn't need any reminders of her foolish behaviour today.

Amanda's stomach roiled every time she thought of Scott and Lola together. Thoughts of her naivete reminded her of the humiliation she had suffered the previous night. After being caught, did that change his plans, or did he take her home? The pain in her chest increased when she envisaged Scott with the other woman.

Steph and Todd stayed at Steph's place last night; was that because they didn't know where Scott had stayed? Whichever way she looked at it, her brother and sister had most likely covered up for Scott's absence at Steph's house last night. Amanda's siblings' betrayal rankled her, and she determined that they needed to come up with a good reason for their absence the previous night.

She recalled the few times she and Scott spent together. How was she to know the kisses meant nothing to him, while for her, they spoke of the commitment to explore the feelings that might grow between them? His touch ignited her, and the smell of him, aftershave and man, sent her senses into a spin. She longed to explore the complex contours of his chest and arms and place kisses on his neck and that square jaw. She had been at the end of his put-downs and teasing for years. When he told Amanda that his behaviour was a way to protect himself from wanting her, Todd's little sister, the excuse now sounded lame, considering his actions last night.

Even after taking a bath and having a light breakfast, she still felt no better. Her side ached, and her heart hurt, too. The dull pain in her stomach was as painful as the ache from the injury. Her eyes, blurry from lack of sleep and bloodshot from crying, added to her misery. When the phone rang, she gritted her teeth, preparing herself for the weak excuses that Todd and Steph could use to justify Scott's

behaviour. The caller was Myra, much to her relief.

"Amanda, how are you? When you shot out of the pub, I was worried, but the security guard said you caught a taxi. Do you want to come here? Your family will want to discuss last night, but if you want to put that off for a short while, spend the day with me."

Amanda packed her bag, thanking her lucky stars; she and Myra had met at her writing course. While she was honing her skills as a proofreader, Myra was expanding her mind, as she laughingly put it. The two girls, older than their classmates, hit it off immediately. When the course finished, they agreed to keep in contact. So far, she had benefited from Myra's kindness and understanding, but she swore to be there should Myra need support.

The familiar drive soothed her, and with her mind concentrating on the trip, she didn't have time to think about the last twenty-four hours. As memories intruded, she pushed them away. Her self-control would last as long as the drive, and when she reached Myra's home, she could work out her plan for dealing with her troubles.

As Todd pulled into the driveway, no one spoke. There was no car at home. The house looked closed up, and Scott was dismayed to discover that Amanda was absent.

"Well, she isn't here. What do we do now?" Steph said.

"Let's see if she left a message."

Scott snorted. "She won't have left a message. If she's not here, then I bet she is with Myra. After last night's tirade, there's no way that woman will tell me if she is with her."

Steph opened the door and called, "Amanda, are you here?"

The silence that greeted her upon entering the house told its own story. Wherever she went, Amanda wasn't interested in hearing excuses or platitudes from any of them. Walking into the kitchen as the boys checked the bedrooms, Steph knew she would find no note.

A knock on the door drew Todd to the front door, only to find their neighbour, Mrs Hoffman, on the front steps. Although they had lived next door for years, the neighbours didn't socialise.

"Todd, dear," Mrs Hoffman said. "I told Amanda I'd pop over to find out how she was today. It was a nasty incident last night. I thought she might want someone to make her a cup of tea or have a chat with her. I guess now you're here, you and your sister can take care of her."

"Ah, sure, except she isn't here. We've just arrived, so I'm not familiar with the incident you mentioned. Would you like to come inside? I will make the tea and can tell us what happened."

When everyone sat in the lounge room, Mrs Hoffman looked from Todd to Steph. "Last night, at ten o'clock, Robert and I were watching the telly. We heard a commotion outside, so Robert hurried to the door to investigate. A woman screamed and cried out for help. Robert recognised Amanda's voice and ran to see if he could help. Bert and Andrew, from across the road, also heard the commotion. When they arrived, they saw a taxi driver trying to force Amanda back into the car after she alighted. The men restrained the driver, and I called triple-O, and the ambulance and police arrived soon after."

The three young people sat stock still, eyes wide and mouths open. Scott made a move first; he rubbed a hand across the back of his neck, and he let out a groan.

"God, this is my fault. Is she hurt?"

Mrs Hoffman's lips pressed together before she said, "When the bloke realised that he ought to leave, he tried to close the back door and caught Amanda with the edge. The ambulance officer gave her painkillers last night."

Steph patted Mrs Hoffman on the arm. "Please thank your husband for going to Amanda's aid. What we need to do now is find her. If I had to guess, I'd say she is visiting her friend, Myra. We'll tell you how she is when we speak to her."

When Mrs Hoffman left, the three at the table looked at each other. Todd shook his head.

"Don't feel special, Scott. We all stuffed up. We could have prevented the attack if we had come home last night instead of going to Steph's house. The question now is, what do we do?"

Steph threw her hands in the air. "I have no idea where Myra lives and don't have a phone number. There is nothing we can do."

Todd gave a wry grin. "I have Myra's number; she gave it to me last night. Give me a minute, and I'll call her."

Chapter 13

When Amanda knocked on the front door, Myra yelled, "Coming!" As she threw open the door, the phone in the hallway rang. She motioned for Amanda to enter while she detoured to answer the phone.

"Yeah, hi, Todd. I guessed you might ring. She arrived a few moments ago. If she wants to talk, she can ring you back later."

Amanda watched as Myra spoke to Todd and heard her friend say, "Sorry, but we all screwed up things. You must show a little patience; we will sort it out."

When Myra hung up, Amanda said, "How did Todd get your phone number?"

"Last night, after you raced out, I was busy telling your ex-boyfriend what a scumbag he was when Todd and a woman walked up to me. Todd introduced me to Steph and himself. We swapped phone numbers in case we needed to contact each other."

Myra noted the overnight bag in her friend's hand. "Are you staying?" she asked.

"I'm not sure. I need to work out what to do, but I'm not rushing into anything yet."

"Todd asked how severe your injury was. Why did he ask that?"

Amanda put her bag down. "Do you want to talk in here or out with the horses?"

"We need to sit and talk."

Amanda sighed, and a shudder passed along her spine as she remembered the night before. As she recounted the taxi driver incident, Myra sat, a dark frown crossing her face. When she finished her tale, Myra groaned.

"Oh, my God, you've had a horrific time of it. Where was your family while this was happening?"

"They didn't show themselves. Most likely, Steph and Todd didn't come to see me because they were unaware of Scott's whereabouts last night and didn't want to tell me. I'm angry because they understood how upset I was, but they did nothing to help. I don't want to talk to them yet."

Myra nodded her head. "I can hold that conversation with Todd if you want me to talk to him. He is still worried about you."

Amanda huffed. "Pity he wasn't concerned last night."

The two girls discussed Scott's behaviour, and Myra provided the tissues and cups of tea. Amanda kept visualising Scott rubbing himself against Lola on the dance floor, and his grip on her bum made the whole thing worse.

When Myra left the house to feed her horses, Amanda sat and considered her siblings' actions. How dare Todd and Steph leave her to her own devices when she left the pub in tears? The pain wasn't receding, and Amanda supposed that the emptiness and the ache in her chest would stay even after the tears subsided. Amanda didn't want to talk to Scott but was angry at Todd and Steph, too. She decided to return home and discuss it with her siblings the next day. Grabbing her bag, Amanda headed out the door. "Myra, I'm going home," she yelled. Myra stuck her head outside the barn and gave her a thumbs-up signal. "Call me if you need me."

Once Myra had finished with the stock, she walked back to the house, her mind turning over possibilities. Amanda hadn't told her not to call Todd, and she fiddled with her mobile as she tried to decide whether to call. Whatever else happened, talking to Todd couldn't make matters worse. With a calming breath, she dialled the phone. A deep male voice answered the phone. "Todd Evans."

"Hi, Todd, Myra here. I rang to tell you what's happening."

"Myra, thanks for that. How is she?"

"Well, you guys messed up in the worst way. Did it not occur to you that Scott's betrayal would devastate Amanda? Why didn't you put your friendship aside for once and help your sister?"

Todd groaned. "I wasn't sure if going home would make matters worse."

"You didn't need to all go. Amanda would have run Scott through with a knife if he had arrived at the house. She was reluctant to talk to Steph in case she said, 'I told you so,' but she would have welcomed you. Anyway, she is on her way home now, and considering what has happened, you would be best advised to leave it until tomorrow before trying to rectify the problem. Oh, and tell Steph from me that 'I told you so' is unkind and unnecessary."

"All right, point taken. What's with the 'I told you so' from Steph?"

"Steph told Amanda that Scott was a player and that he would hurt her. Even if she's right, it doesn't make it any better for her."

When Myra ended the call, Todd reflected on what she had said. His reaction to the call was to jump into the car and race to Amanda's place, but Myra's warning rang in his ears. God, they had messed up badly. Scott had broken his little sister's heart, and he and Steph had taken the easy way out by leaving her to her own devices.

Chapter 14

After spending the morning with Myra, Amanda felt better talking to her siblings. She never intended to speak to Scott again, but needed to tell Todd and Steph what happened on her night out. Unwilling to converse with her brother and sister that day, she kept her return home quiet.

The house looked the same, but the cups rinsed on the draining board showed that her brother, sister, and Scott had visited. God knows what Scott thought he could say to improve the circumstances. Amanda heated the leftovers and settled in to watch TV with a cup of tea in one hand and a plate in the other.

Disgusted with the viewing choices, Amanda decided to listen to the radio for company. The television shows comprised cooking shows, reality challenges, and the news. Love song after love song was the programmer's choice, and the sad lyrics of the songs brought tears to her eyes. In the silence that filled the room after shutting off the radio, Amanda kept seeing Scott and Lola rubbing against each other as they danced.

When Amanda told him she was going out for a girls' night, he asked where they were going. She could not give him their venue because Myra had organised the booking. If he had known where they were going, would he have chosen a different pub and a woman with whom to spend the night? Damn it! Steph had told her he was a player, but she had thought his approaches to her were genuine. Did he intend to continue his pursuit of her while sleeping with any girl who gave him the eye?

Drained of energy and wishing to forget last night's farce, Amanda bathed and climbed into bed. Sleep didn't come fast; she tossed and turned as she relived the awful night. After what seemed like hours, Amanda gave up trying to sleep. She climbed out of bed and padded through the dark house on her way to the kitchen. Amanda flipped on the light as a strange noise sounded from the hallway. When she approached the sound, she saw the doorknob move; someone was trying to enter the house. The blood froze in her veins, and her heart beat faster. The door rattled in its frame as the intruder tried to gain access. Amanda fled to her bedroom.

Once she had locked the door, she looked for something to stop the trespasser from entering her room if he broke the flimsy lock. Her eyes fell on a pair of thongs discarded next to the bed. She wedged her thongs under the door as the sound of breaking glass filtered through to her room.

Amanda rushed into the ensuite, grabbing an aerosol deodorant and a room freshener canister. If the intruder made it this far, he would get an eyeful, and while it wasn't mace, it should slow his approach. Amanda dialled Triple O and babbled out her story to the dispatcher. The woman told her to stay on the line, and Amanda hung on, praying for a police car to arrive.

As the assailant bashed on the bedroom door, she clenched her fists. He continued to pound, without success, at the sturdy door. Shaking, she sobbed, "He's trying to get into the bedroom!" she said to the dispatcher.

"They're nearly there, just around the corner. Hold on, darl, you'll be okay."

When the sounds of a siren pierced the air, the intruder shouted, "I might not get my payment tonight, but I'll be back bitch; you can count on it." The pounding stopped as footsteps echoed through the house.

"Police! Stay where you are." Amanda listened as doors opened and shut, and a sharp rap on her door made her jump.

"Police, open the door!"

"Wait."

Amanda struggled to pull the wedges out from under the door. Her shaking fingers couldn't grasp the wedged thongs she used to help keep the intruder out. Her voice wavered. "I can't move the wedges I jammed under the door."

A male voice cursed. "Take a deep breath and try again."

She did as the police officer said. While not wholly steady, her fingers hooked around the flip-flops and the door released. When she turned the key in the lock, the door burst open.

"Ah, we meet again," said the police officer from the previous night. "Tell me what's going on here."

Amanda's body convulsed, and she swayed on her feet. Her eyes welled, and a single tear slid down her face. A firm hand gripped her, and she sat her in a chair.

"Take deep breaths. You'll feel better in a minute."

She gave a shaky laugh. "Glad you think so. Can I call my brother?"

"I need a statement, but you can ring your brother first."

Amanda dialled Todd's cell, but remembered that both Todd and Steph turned their phones off at night. Clenching her jaw, she pressed the speed dial for Scott and listened as it rang. After a few rings, he answered. "Mandy?"

"Scott, I need you to wake Todd. I've had an intruder, and the police are here." There was a break in her voice, and then a male voice said, "Sir, I am Constable Thomas from the Westbourne Police. Your sister needs support. How soon can you get here?" After listening to Scott's answer, the constable ended the call. She didn't bother to correct the police officer's assumption that he was her brother. Todd would arrive soon, and the police officer would work out the relationship.

The police had finished their questions when Scott arrived.

"Now that your brother is here, I can leave you. We haven't caught the intruder, but we can identify him. Try to board up that broken window, and if I were you, I'd install a security system."

Amanda wrapped her shaking hands around herself. Despite her distress, she managed a snarky comment.

"You might have caught him if you hadn't arrived with your sirens blaring. What did you think he would do when he heard them?"

"Yeah, that was a tactical error. We will catch the bloke, but you need to be careful."

"How is this man walking around after he assaulted Mandy two nights ago?" Scott asked.

The police officer sighed. "We catch the culprits, and the judges release them. It doesn't seem to matter what the criminal does. The system is bogged down with rules that make it easier to put people out on bail. Install a security system and exercise caution. We'll let you know as soon as we catch him."

Chapter 15

When Amanda called, Scott wasn't sure what to say, but by the time the police officer finished speaking, he was hunting for his keys. Unable to sleep, he had been roaming the house, still dressed. He had considered waking Todd, but figured it was faster if he didn't have to wake his mate and then wait for him to get ready.

As he stood looking at Amanda, he could see the stress of the night on her face. She was pasty white, her blue eyes huge in her pale face, and tears spilled down her cheeks. Her arms, wrapped around herself, were still shaking. He stepped towards her and said, "Come here, sweetie."

Scott's warm embrace wrapped around her, and Amanda's tears became sobs as she buried her face against his shoulder. With her fists clutching the soft material of his shirt, she hung on to him as if her life depended on it. He patted her on the back and made soothing noises. With a hiccoughing breath, she pulled away.

"What are you doing here? I wanted Todd, not you."

"Yeah, but you know how hard it is to wake Todd, and I hadn't gone to bed. I wasn't sure if you needed someone fast, so I came."

"Well, now you can leave. I don't need you."

Scott stared at her in disbelief. "So, you want me to leave you in a house that has a broken front panel and is easy access for the nut job the police haven't found? Sure, I can do that."

He held his breath as he walked towards the door; Amanda sobbed again. "Scott, please don't leave me. I'm scared."

Releasing the breath, he returned to her side. "I need to board up that hole; while I do, pack a bag. You can't stay here tonight; we can work out better security tomorrow."

"You know I hate you?"

"Yeah, I get that. Can we discuss that after we leave here?"

Amanda remained silent as she walked towards her room. Once Scott boarded up the hole, he escorted her towards his car. As they drove through the dark streets of Westbourne, Scott made Amanda feel safe. The truth, she admitted to herself, was that she still loved him but hated what he had done to her. Her eyes drooped, and he said, "Sleep for a few minutes. I'll wake you when we get there." Taking him at his word, she closed her eyes.

The car stopped, and the lack of movement jolted Amanda awake. Eyes wide and heart pounding, she looked around her. "Easy, Mandy. You're safe."

The soothing voice calmed her, and she turned to Scott.

"Where are we?"

"At the Southern Arms. I rang ahead and booked a room. I need to leave you to get the key. Will you be alright?"

Amanda frowned and clamped her jaws together.

Once Scott had parked the car, Amanda alighted with her small bag. Scott returned with the key and opened the door to the room. The unit was a single room with a small kitchen and a solitary double bed.

"Why are we here? It would be best if you took me back to Steph's place. I am not sleeping here with you."

He ran his hand over the back of his neck; he looked at her with sadness.

"Mandy, consider it for a moment. I don't believe anyone followed us, but do you want to draw that nut job to Steph's house? I can sleep on the couch or get another room. I thought you'd feel better if you weren't alone."

Amanda launched herself at Scott, hitting and scratching like a feral cat. She pummelled him with clenched fists.

"Damn you, you bastard. How can you make me think you care and then pick up that floozy in the pub? What were you going to do? Were you going to have a meaningful relationship with me while screwing anyone who made themselves available? I thought you cared for me, but I was an amusement while you waited for some action, wasn't I? You disgust me."

Amanda paced back and forth in the small space. She shot Scott a repulsed look.

"What, cat got your tongue? Can't you think of one good reason you had to hit on that slut? How would you feel if you discovered I was all over a guy on the dance floor like you were? You practically had sex on the dance floor; the only thing that prevented that from happening was that you were both wearing clothes."

As Scott approached, she waved her hands in a halt signal."Please don't come near me, and don't touch me. I want nothing to do with you. Sleep anywhere you want, but not with me."

With her tirade ended, an overwhelming sensation of tiredness assailed her. She sank onto the bed and watched Scott as he sat in the lone armchair in the room. His head dropped, and his shoulders slumped. When he moved, he ran his hands through his hair; he held his hand up in appeal.

"Mandy, I didn't sleep with her. I went there looking for action because I was frustrated trying to move our relationship to the next level. Every time I got you alone, Steph interrupted. I'm unsure if it was intentional, but it was inopportune."

Turning to face Scott, Amanda pointed out, "It was intentional. Steph told me you were a player and would break my heart if I got involved with you. A damn good analysis, wasn't it?" She watched him as he struggled to gain control. Her body betrayed her even when her mind told her that this man was wrong for her. His proximity made her heart race and her skin heat. The need to reach out and touch him was overwhelming, and she had to sit on her hands to stop herself from reaching for him.

Scott slammed his fist on the kitchen counter.

"Damn it, Mandy! You've never been an amusement, although you have been a distraction. I've spent the last four weeks in a constant state of arousal, and I figured if Steph wouldn't let me get to you, then I had to look elsewhere. I want you, not a pick-up in a bar. How don't you understand that?"

"The evidence states otherwise. Why didn't we go away? It wouldn't have been too hard to take off for a few days, but no, you have dance sex with that slut at the pub, and you were in such a hurry to get into her pants that you practically hauled her out of the room."

"Do you have short-term memory loss, woman? I organised for us to leave for a few days, and your brother and sister jumped at the chance to chaperone us."

Amanda slumped onto the bed, and her head dropped. Her defeated demeanour tugged at Scott's heart.

He sat on the edge of the bed. "Us screaming at each other won't solve the problem. I'm sorry; I'm sorrier than you can ever imagine. I screwed up, and I'll have to live with that, but at the moment, we should concentrate on you staying safe."

When she yawned again, Scott stood.

"You need to sleep. I can sleep on the couch, or if you'd prefer, I can rouse the owner and move to another room. You choose."

Amanda fiddled with the edge of the doona. She didn't want him in another room, but she didn't know if she could fall asleep with him just a few meters away. With a loud sigh, she conceded and asked him to stay. While he collected a sheet and an extra pillow from the cupboard, she settled down and closed her eyes.

Chapter 16

Someone was banging on the door. As Amanda watched, the door bowed inwards. She cast a desperate look at the wedges, and to her horror, she realised they wouldn't hold. Screaming in terror, someone had a firm grip on her arms. As she flailed around, trying to dislodge her attacker, his grip tightened. "Wake up, Mandy; you're dreaming."

Amanda snapped out of her nightmare at the sound of Scott's voice. Her entire body was shaking, and she couldn't stop the sobs that wracked her body.

Scott pulled her onto his lap and cradled her. He rocked her and murmured soothing words. As her self-control returned, the sobs stopped. Wrapped in his arms, she was safe, but the hard planes of his thighs under her made her tingle and fluster. Not wanting to end this embrace, she remained seated on his lap.

Steph's warning rang through Amanda's head. When her body stopped shaking, she turned her head to tell him he could let her go, but the hungry expression in his eyes robbed her of speech. He ran his hands through her hair and cupped her cheek. His touch soothed her, but the desire in his eyes told a different story. But as Steph insisted, if he were a player, why did he keep returning for her? Did she listen to Steph or trust her instincts?

Amanda leaned forward and placed a kiss on Scott's mouth. His arm around her tightened, and he deepened the kiss. Scott nipped her bottom lip and then soothed it with his tongue. As he ran his tongue over her lips, she opened her mouth for him. He invaded her mouth, his tongue tasting and duelling with hers. With a groan, he swung her around, and suddenly she was astride him.

Amanda was hot and needy, unsure how far Scott intended to take this. As though reading her mind, he pulled back and held her away from him, his hands placed on her forearms.

"Mandy, if you don't want to end up in that bed underneath me, we had better stop now."

Passion battled with good sense. Did she trust Scott enough to take this further? The pain of his betrayal still sat like a weight on her chest. Scott's kiss made her light-headed, stoking her craving for him into a raging inferno. Despite what had gone before, didn't she deserve one night with Scott?

She looked him in the eyes and then licked her lips. She ran her hand up and down his bare arm and then undid the buttons on his shirt. When he covered her hand with his and stopped her progress, she rolled her hips and rubbed herself against the hard bulge in his jeans. They both groaned. His breath was uneven and ragged, and his voice was rough. "Mandy, you're killing me."

Amanda raised an eyebrow. Her face flushed, and as she ran her hand over his unfastened shirt, she said: "What's the matter, Butch? Do you need an engraved invitation?" Scott stood up, almost tipping her off his lap. She shrieked as he grabbed her and dumped her on the bed.

"Don't call me Butch," he snarled.

"Why, what will you do to me if I do?" she taunted, fluttering her eyelashes at him, femme fatale style.

"I'll think of something," he said as he pulled his shirt over his head and unbuttoned the top of his jeans.

Just the sight of his bare chest made Amanda short of breath, and her words stuck in her throat. God, he was gorgeous! As Scott approached the bed, the look in his eyes almost turned her into a puddle on the mattress. When he lowered himself onto the bed, his weight pushed the bedding down, and she rolled closer to him.

"Wait," she said.

She heard him swear under his breath, and he said, "What?"

"I don't share," she said, glaring at him. "Never, under any circumstances, and I won't play nice."

Scott grinned. "Not sharing is a given, and when you want to play dirty, I'll be right there with you. Now, let's remove your clothes; you're wearing too many things for the punishment I have in mind."

She gasped as Scott ran his hands under her tank top and palmed her breasts. "Help me out here, Mandy."

Amanda groaned. "Take your hands off me if you want help with the clothes."

"Stuff that," he said as he pushed up her top and lavished her breasts with licks and nips. When she was writhing, mindless with desire, he pulled her shirt off and then slid her shorts and knickers off together. As he stepped back to remove his jeans, he spent a few minutes gazing at her. Amanda was self-conscious and tried to cover herself with her hands, but he growled at her. "Don't try to hide from me, sweetheart; you're gorgeous."

All Amanda could feel when Scott returned to bed was the silky skin that covered his finely honed muscles. The longing in his eyes left her in no doubt: he wanted her as much as she wanted him.

Chapter 17

Amanda woke slowly. She was content and restored. Too relaxed to roll over, she reached out her hand to touch Scott; the other side of the bed was cold and empty. As she listened to the silence in the room, she was sure he was not there. Pulling herself out of bed, she stumbled to the bathroom. Previously unused muscles protested at her movement. The twinges made her smile; they reminded her of the night she had spent with Scott. When she reached the bathroom, she saw his toiletries lined up on the top of the cabinet next to hers. There had been a touch of concern that he had left. Confident now that he had gone out to get food, she climbed into the shower.

Scott knocked on the bathroom door.

"I got breakfast for us, and then we need to go home. Todd and Steph are worrying about you for different reasons, though. We need to work on security for the house, too, and it wouldn't be a bad idea if Steph did the same."

Once they had had breakfast, they headed home. Scott phoned Todd to suggest that he and Steph meet at Amanda's house to work out a strategy together. Amanda was a little nervous about Steph's reaction to her relationship with Scott, but she couldn't work up the energy to care after last nig

When she walked through the front door with the piece of wood covering the broken glass, it gave her a shock, and for a moment, sickness assailed her. Scott placed his arm around her and gave her a gentle squeeze. "We'll sort this mess out soon. The police are staking out his property; they think the taxi bloke is responsible for a few attacks in nearby suburbs. With some new security devices installed, you will be in no danger here, even if you live alone." A question bubbled in her mind, but she pushed it aside. Now was not the time to work out where this relationship was going.

Todd walked to the back of the house and entered through the kitchen door. Steph followed close behind, while Todd headed straight for his sister, and Steph walked towards Scott. Amanda watched through the corner of her eye while reassuring Todd that she was okay.

Steph launched a tirade at Scott as soon as she was close to him. "Damn you, Scott! You can't keep your hands to yourself, can you? I bet you slept with her while you protected her from a madman; who was protecting her from you? What happens now? You get bored and move on, and we get to pick up the pieces again."

As she disentangled herself from her brother's hug, Amanda moved to stand next to Scott. He took her hand in his. "Don't argue with your sister over me. I'm willing to take the blame."

She shook her head. "There is no blame to apportion here. Steph, I love you, but mind your own bloody business. Your actions prevented us from getting together, culminating in that incident at the pub. I understand that you're unhappy about us being together. If it doesn't work out, I promise not to cry on your shoulder."

"Aren't we focusing on the wrong thing here? Amanda's home invasion should be a priority here. Grab a seat and give us the details, sis," Todd said. When she finished retelling the intruder incident, Scott spoke. "You two came in the back door. Did you see the front entrance?"

Steph shook her head. "No. Did the guy gain entry through the front door?"

"Yep. I've got security suggestions for the house, and when we finish here, we need to look at your place, Steph," Scott said.

"I'm not in any danger, am I?"

Todd agreed with Scott. "You can't be too careful now that this bloke is targeting Amanda. What happens if he can't reach her because of the security measures we have in place here? He may come looking for an alternative way to pay her back."

"Let's get someone here to give us some suggestions. We should either remove the glass panel next to the front door or consider reversing the door's orientation. That may be how they constructed front entrances back when Mum and Dad built the house, but now it's a security risk."

Later that afternoon, a security consultant assessed the house. He suggested that they should turn the door around. If they removed the glass panel, the hallway would be too dark, but the proximity of the door locks to the glass was unacceptable. If they turned the door around, the bolts would not be accessible even if someone broke the window again. The consultant suggested that Amanda fit a security screen on the front door and one at the back. The technician was to install a security system covering the front and rear doors, as well as the windows.

"Grab a bag and some clothes, Mandy. We will not stay here until the security systems are fully operational. No point putting you in unnecessary danger."

"Do you want to stay at my place?" Steph asked.

Amanda shook her head. "No, Scott thought, if someone is watching me, we don't want to draw this guy towards your place. We'll find a motel and keep moving until we make the house safe. We shouldn't be on the move for more than two days."

Chapter 18

Scott and Amanda spent an idyllic few days together; as they moved from motel to motel, eating out and spending time together was a dream come true for Amanda. With no interruptions from concerned siblings, they got reacquainted. While they were antagonistic toward each other for most of their lives, living in the same house meant they understood each other well. Scott's trip overseas with Todd had changed his viewpoint of the world, and she was relishing the chance to get to know him again.

A phone call from the security firm brought them back to earth. They needed to go home. The repairs and safety upgrades at her house were complete, and Todd had organised the security measures at Steph's house; now, the girls need not fear intruders.

They had just arrived home when Scott's phone rang; the screen identified the caller as Todd. With his phone against his ear, he walked away from where Amanda was sitting. "What's up, mate?

"Scott, we must tell the girls about our career choice soon. There are only two weeks left."

As he ran his hand across his face, Scott conceded Todd had a point. "I've been enjoying my time with Mandy. Once we tell the girls, that will end."

"Yeah, well, mate, you can't tell her as you walk out the door. Best we do it soon; they will both need the chance to adjust to the change."

Scott rubbed his chin and sighed. "We'll come for a drive. Maybe we can eat dinner and then give them the news."

Scott walked back to Amanda's office. When he put his hand on her neck and squeezed, she shuddered. "Don't distract me again, Butch. I need to finish this work, or I'll get fired."

"You understand what happens when you call me Butch? I'll punish you, and that could take hours before I'm sure you're repentant."

She giggled. "As appealing as that thought is, I need to work."

"Okay, can we go to Steph's for dinner if I leave you to work? Todd and I need to talk to you both."

Amanda worked for the next three hours. She put her work aside as she and Scott moved around, but now she needed to edit the manuscripts her agent had sent. Now and then, a word or phrase would distract her, and her thoughts returned to Scott. He was like a fever that burned inside her. She loved spending time with him, both in and out of bed. He was funny, irreverent, and so sexy that she needed to pinch herself to check that it wasn't a dream.

She took a break once she had worked her way through her emails and prioritised the waiting documents. She found him stretched out on the couch, watching television.

"Hey, sweetie, are you finished?"

As she dropped to the couch beside Scott's outstretched legs, Amanda said, "I've sorted the stuff I need to start on first. Tomorrow, if you and Todd need buddy time, I can start on the papers I've sorted. I guess I've been monopolising you, but he's had you for years."

Scott hooked his arm around her waist and pulled her down. So she lay on top of him. "You can monopolise me some more if you want."

She smiled and bent to kiss him on the mouth. When he attempted to deepen the kiss, she sat back. "Oh no, you don't! You'll blame me when we don't get to Steph's place on time. On your feet, my love. You have secret men's business to do."

"Do you want to come and lie here with me if I promise not to blame you?"

Amanda sighed. "Yes, I want to come and lie with you, but you told Todd we would be there for dinner. We'll be cutting it fine."

Scott swung his legs around and sat up. "You make a compelling argument, but we aren't finished. I'll take a rain check for now."

Chapter 19

Amanda loved Steph's place. The acreage lot that was Steph's backyard overlooked the hills and neighbouring properties. The wide veranda at the back of the house was ideal for afternoon barbecues and drinks. As expected, they found Steph and Todd lounging in the squatter's chairs near the railing when they arrived.

"Ah, the lovebirds have joined the mortal folk," Todd joked.

"It took lots of organising to get Mandy alone, mate. First, I had to disgrace myself, and I had to hire a deranged taxi driver to cause anguish and fear. You should be honoured by our arrival."

After Todd had dispensed the drinks to the newcomers, the men started the barbecue, and the chatter turned to general topics. Amanda could sense an undercurrent of tension between Scott and Todd, but she bided her time. She realised the men had something brewing and were reluctant to share their news. She prayed they wouldn't have to travel back overseas for another year.

Dinner passed quickly, and the conversation was wide-ranging. Steph brought up the intruder. "Do you believe this guy has stopped with his revenge?"

Todd shook his head. "I'd love to say yes, but I fear that his type of madness doesn't fade away. He's waiting for the right time, so we must show vigilance."

"Yeah, ladies. Don't slack off on the alarms or the door locks, even during the day. There's nothing to say he will return at night. This guy could return during daylight because a taxi doesn't cause suspicion amongst residents," Scott agreed.

When Amanda returned the plates to the kitchen, Scott offered to load the dishwasher. Once he completed the task, he wrapped his arm around her shoulders. "Why so quiet?"

"I'm waiting for you and Todd to drop your bombshell. I'm sure Steph can tell something is amiss with you two, and the sooner you put us out of our misery, the better."

Scott pulled her into his arms and kissed her. "My little detective. Yeah, we have something to tell you, but the news will upset you, and we're cowards when it comes to causing you two pain."

She placed her palms on his chest. "Maybe the reality won't be as horrid as we imagine. Get it over with, please."

On the veranda, Steph and Todd were engrossed in a deep discussion. Scott grinned at Todd. "Why did we fool ourselves into thinking they wouldn't guess something is happening with us?"

"It's called women's intuition," Steph said.

"Besides that, we understand you two so well that you have no hope of hiding something from us," Amanda added. Scott patted his knee. "Come and sit with me, sweetie."

"What, when I hear your news, I'll run away screaming?"

"Yeah, it's a possibility. Come here."

With Amanda seated next to Scott, the men looked at each other. "You or me?" Todd asked. "You start, and I'll butt in," replied Scott.

Todd took a deep breath and then began. "When we went overseas, it was to see the world and travel before we settled. The things we saw gave us a different perspective on life."

Scott interjected. "We've had a cushy life, but many people have no food or security or are living in danger because of the unrest in their countries."

Todd continued. "We decided we should give something back to the world. Neither of us would make good missionaries, but we agreed that joining the army could allow us to participate in humanitarian activities."

Both sisters sat, immobilised by the news. Amanda's face had gone white, and her eyes welled with tears. Steph, her eyes wide, shook her head. Neither of the girls said a word, and Todd and Scott watched as emotions chased across their faces. Amanda gave a loud sob and pushed herself away from Scott. The door banged behind her as she entered the house, and the sound of the front door slamming mobilised him. When Amanda and Scott disappeared, Steph said,

"Great bombshell, bro. I'm not sure what to say. Are you aware that people die in the army? It's not all honour and righteousness."

"That is why we put off telling you. We realised it would upset you, especially Amanda, after what happened to Jake. Sometimes, a person must do what they think is right, even if it causes others pain."

"I need a hug," Steph said. Todd stood and pulled her towards him, his arms wrapped around her, and he heard a sob. He rubbed his hand over her back and attempted to soothe his sister's fears.

Scott caught Amanda as she headed for the driveway. He reached out and grabbed her, and she swung around with her fist and punched him in the chest. The tears flowed, and her hair was wild, as though she had been pushing it away from her face as she fled. She cocked her other fist, and he grabbed her hands. "You killing me, Mandy, will not improve things. Talk to me, sweetie."

"Talk to you? Jake died, remember? What if you or Todd dies?"

"Darl, Jake was an idiot. He took risks, and he died. He didn't die because of something the army did; you can't blame them for his speeding and losing control of a vehicle. Todd and I will follow orders and do our best to keep ourselves safe. We both want to come home."

"How can you do this? We've just got together, and you're going to leave."

"Todd and I applied as soon as we got home. The recruitment procedure takes some time to complete, and we will need to wait until they have an intake process in place. I didn't know we would work things out. When I applied to go, I hoped to solve the problem between us; I would be out of your hair and doing something worthwhile. Please, Mandy, don't give up on me. We can work this out."

She stepped into his embrace. "Damn you, Scott! You've caused me more heartache than any man has a right to. Why do I still care?"

"All I can say is thank god you do."

Once Amanda was calmer, he led her back to the house where Todd and Steph sat. Amanda walked over to her brother, and he extended his arms, so she hugged him. As he tucked a strand of hair back behind her ear, he kissed her on the forehead. "I'm sorry, sis. I understand that this upsets you, but we must do this. I don't expect Steph and you to understand, but Scott and I have taken a long time to make this decision. It's the right thing for us to do."

Chapter 20

Amanda didn't understand what happened. One minute, she was living her dream, and the next, both men had left her. Ten weeks! Seventy days! It sounded like a lifetime. While she and Steph continued their lives, the boys would be so tired and busy that they wouldn't have time to think of the women they left behind.

The sisters researched online the training course that the recruits did. They knew the training conducted at Kapooka was just outside Wagga Wagga. They investigated leave times and contact opportunities, and read the information on the training the men had to endure each week.

It was four weeks before Todd or Scott got local leave, and there were restrictions on the areas of the township of Wagga Wagga they could frequent. Steph and Amanda made tentative bookings at the Astra motel, one of the motels in the designated location, and checked flight availability. Neither wanted to miss the opportunity to visit.

Their research found that letters were the lifeblood of soldiers, and even if they didn't have time to answer, messages from home were always welcome. Both girls wrote letters to Scott and Todd each week, and, as suggested, they dated and numbered them in case the mail was delayed.

Sunday night phone calls were the only time Amanda spoke to her brother and boyfriend. She made sure there were no whines regarding how much she missed them and concentrated on sounding upbeat and happy. At the end of each call, she felt both happy and sad.

The training period passed more quickly than Amanda had believed possible. There was an opportunity to visit on four weekends and a bonus of a Sunday church service where she and Steph could sit with the men. When the march invitations were sent out, Amanda was excited. The end of the training period did not mean that Todd and Scott could go home; it meant they would be transferred elsewhere for further training.

The day of the marching out dawned sunny and hot. Amanda and Steph made up part of a large group of friends, relatives, and girlfriends who received invitations to watch the men and women of the brigade become soldiers. The march past was impressive, and the soldiers looked a picture in their dress uniforms. The sheer joy at their success became apparent when, after being dismissed, they threw their hats in the air.

As the soldiers scattered, the women searched the group for Scott and Todd. Todd reached them first and hugged them. He was so handsome in his uniform that Amanda's breath whooshed out of her lungs. "God, Todd, you look wonderful. If you weren't my brother, I'd be chasing you everywhere."

"Well, just be grateful he's your brother, or I'd need to beat him," a deep voice growled. Amanda squealed and spun around. She launched herself at him, and he caught her in the air. "Oh god, oh god, you're here. I've missed you so much. We don't have lots of time together, do we?"

"No, but we can see you tomorrow at church."

Amanda laughed. "You two have never been to church as much as you have over the last ten weeks."

"If it means I get to spend time with you, sweetheart, then I'll become a devout churchgoer."

Chapter 21

After the excitement of the march out, Amanda was depressed and miserable. She had enjoyed the ceremony and the time spent with Todd and Scott, but she could see no way for her and Scott to continue as a couple. He and Todd started training at the Enoggera base, where Scott was a transport person and Todd was an engineer, utilising his civilian qualifications. They were so busy that they barely managed regular phone calls. While Enoggera was closer to Westbourne than Kapooka, it may have been the end of the earth. She needed to talk to Scott about relocating. She didn't want him to feel she was crowding him, but she needed more contact with him.

Amanda broached the subject during a phone call the next day. She could do her job anywhere, so her location wasn't imperative.

"It doesn't matter where I live; I can do my work wherever there is an internet connection."

She heard Scott sigh over the phone. "I sometimes leave the base for days on end. The Army uses different vehicles for supply distribution, which means travelling."

"But being alone there wouldn't be any different from being here alone. If I live nearby, you can spend your downtime with me. Please, Scott, I don't want to nag, but I miss you."

Amanda's move to the outskirts of Brisbane went without a hitch. She missed her hometown, but the community feel in the suburb of Enoggera was strong. The residents ranged from older couples to families and professionals. The proximity to the central business district and public transport made the suburb popular with professionals and workers. She found herself drawn into activities that she had never participated in while living in Westbourne. Morning walks became part of her day, and she frequented the various parks and bike trails that were part of the suburb's charm.

Having Scott and Todd close by made the relocation worthwhile. Often, Steph joined them on the weekends, and it was as if they were transporting their home to the city. Things frequently changed for Scott and Todd as they moved around for courses or did their duties. Twelve months after their enlistment, Scott and Todd arrived at the house with grim looks.

"Bad day at the office, boys?" Amanda quipped. When neither of them answered her, she scrutinised their faces. Scott wrapped his arm around her waist and pulled her in close for a hug. "Mandy, the army is deploying the unit. You need to pack up the house and head home to Westbourne."

This statement was the last thing Amanda expected Scott to say. It took a moment or two for the import of the words to register. She blinked at him and said,

"Why? How long does this posting last?"

Todd joined the conversation at that point. "Amanda, it lasts for six months, and even though we should be there as peacekeepers, in a non-combat role, things can go wrong. I agree with Scott; you need to go home."

"When do you leave?"

"We have a month, and they will give us time to say goodbye, but it's best if you move straight away while Scott and I can help," Todd said.

Scott and Todd were busy preparing for their unit's deployment. Not only did they have to pack away personal items, but their vaccinations needed updating. While they filled their time with last-minute details, it didn't stop Scott from second-guessing himself. He questioned the wisdom of starting a relationship with Amanda and was torn about what to do. Even though he tossed around different scenarios, he couldn't come up with a solution to the problem. Scott sat in front of the TV, too distracted to watch any programs playing. As he stared into space, he was oblivious to Todd's presence.

"Scott, what are you thinking?"

When Scott didn't answer, Todd pushed his feet off the coffee table. A low growl was the only response.

"It's obvious; you have something on your mind. Do you want to discuss whatever is distracting you?"

Scott sighed. "I'm thinking about this deployment and wondering whether I did the right thing by starting a relationship with Amanda. Now, I have the responsibility for someone else's feelings. I shouldn't have hooked up with her."

"Well, that ship has sailed. You can't undo the past, and you can't protect her from hurt, just the pain you might cause her. The girls understand we will be in a dangerous country, but this time, at least, it ought to be reasonably safe."

"But what about the bigger hurts?" Scott asked as he paced.

"What do you mean by bigger hurts?"

"What happens if I get killed in an accident or disabled and have to return home in a wheelchair?"

"If you get killed, the three of us will mourn, but in time, we'll move on with our lives. If a disability confined you to a wheelchair, we would be sad for you but grateful that you hadn't died. You can't protect the people you love from the pain of loving someone. What if Amanda had an accident while we weren't here? Would you blame her for causing you distress?"

Scott ran his hand across the back of his neck. He stopped pacing and stared at Todd. "What happens when married guys go overseas? We've seen the reunions. The man leaves a pregnant wife and returns to a three- or four-month-old baby who doesn't recognise him. The woman with the toddler in her arms sends her husband off, but when he returns, his kid hides behind the mother because he doesn't remember his father."

Todd rubbed a hand over his face. "Amanda is neither pregnant nor the mother of a toddler, and until you do the right thing by her, she is not a wife. I don't understand why we're even having this conversation. Do you think I should disown Steph and Amanda so they won't be distressed if something were to happen to me? Your theory is flawed, and stressing about something you can't change is pointless."

"Maybe you're right, but I'm not convinced."

"Why don't you discuss this with 'Manda and let her decide what she wants?"

Scott pinched his nose and ran his hands through his blond hair. Todd had an uneasy suspicion that they hadn't resolved the problem.

Chapter 22

Amanda surveyed the boxes lined up along the lounge room wall. The removers stacked the cartons and left her to sort out the large marked boxes. A knock at the door drew her attention away from the packing cases. When she opened the door, her eyes lit up as she greeted her neighbour, Mrs Hoffman.

"Hello, dear. We noticed you were back; I wanted to come over and say welcome. We missed you while you were away." Amanda smiled at her neighbour and clasped her hand. "Thanks, Mrs Hoffman. It's good to be back."

"I'll just let you get on with the unpacking, but if you need something, remember we are just next door."

Mrs Hoffman walked to the door and then turned back. "I nearly forgot to tell you. The nice police officer who came the night of the incident asked me to inform you that they have caught that man. He attacked other young women, and the police could tie those in thanks to the information you gave them."

Amanda smiled. "That's great; thanks for letting me know."

As she surveyed the boxes again, the back-screen door banged, and a voice yelled, "Manda, where are you?" Amanda laughed. "Steph, the house isn't that big. I'm in the lounge room." When Steph entered the room, she gazed at the boxes and let out a groan.

"How could you accumulate so much stuff in such a short time? I guess you want a hand. Where do you want to start?"

The girls worked through the morning, and by lunchtime, everything was away. Amanda ordered a pizza, and after the delivery boy left, she and Steph sat on the shady patio. She scrutinised the foliage; it needed a trim, and other plants looked worse for their neglect. At first, she had considered renting the house while she was away, but knowing the potential damage that tenants could cause convinced her that leaving it vacant was a better choice.

Her relocation was unexpected, and she could move immediately because there were no tenants to evict.

Steph grabbed a large slice of the pizza and eyed her sister. "How do you feel about the boys going overseas?"

"I knew it might happen, and they say it's in a humanitarian project, but I can't help but worry. Not seeing either Todd or Scott for another six months is awful. It's like when they were away last time. I worry about them and miss them. With my relationship with Scott working out, I'm worried that he'll meet someone else or decide he can live without me. Is that foolish of me?"

Steph wiped her mouth with a napkin and shook her head. "No, it's not foolish. I worry, too, and if I were sending my boyfriend away for six months, I'd have the same concerns as you. All we can do is keep them thinking about us with letters and parcels. We might even manage to Skype them sometimes."

Amanda brightened. "Yeah, I never considered Skype. If we can see them sometimes, it will make the time go faster."

Amanda filled her days by catching up with friends and getting the garden in order. She had no contact with Todd or Scott and assumed they were too busy preparing for their trip to talk to either her or Steph.

The university and college assignments she edited slowed down as the term drew to a close. At various times of the year, she became inundated with the work of students who hadn't paid enough attention in primary school to edit their written tasks. Spellcheck eliminated most of the fundamental errors, and her job was to make the rest presentable. While there was still book editing work to be done, none of the manuscripts called to her, and she decided she needed a break.

After a quick call to Myra, Amanda packed an overnight bag, including her riding gear. It had been ages since they'd ridden together, but she decided she would remember enough of the basic rules not to fall off. Myra was excited to have Amanda visit, and the girls had lots of catching up to do.

"What about a ride and a talk, Amanda? It's a lovely day; it seems a pity to waste it sitting inside," Myra suggested.

For the first half of the ride, there wasn't much talk. The girls put the horses through their paces, and riders and their mounts worked up a sweat. Once they turned the horses for home, the girls chatted, reins loose on their necks. There was a lot to discuss and almost a year's worth of information.

"What are Scott and Todd doing with themselves? Something must have changed for you to come home," Myra said.

"Yeah, the boys are being deployed. There's no point in my staying at Enoggera while they are not there. It's supposed to be a humanitarian mission, but that doesn't mean Steph and I will stop worrying until they get home," she replied.

As they cooled their horses, Amanda's phone rang. The screen said 'Scott', so she answered with anticipation.

"Scott, hi. How's it going in sunny Brisbane?"

The gruff voice that made her tingle answered. "I wouldn't know. I'm in suburban Westbourne, looking for my girl."

Amanda squealed, and then Scott's laugh rumbled through the phone.

"How soon can you come home?"

"Myra and I went for a ride. Maybe I can return in forty minutes once we clean the horses and turn them out."

"Okay, I'll see you then.

Chapter 23

The trip home was both exciting and tinged with sorrow. Amanda hadn't seen Scott in three or four weeks, so spending time with him now was priceless. The pain that shadowed Scott's visit was the knowledge that this was the last time she could see him for six months or more. Amanda pushed aside her negative thoughts as she alighted from her car and sprinted up the driveway. As she entered the patio, Scott stood up and grabbed her as she threw herself at him. His arms tightened around her, and he pressed his nose to her hair to smell the lavender shampoo she used. "God. I've missed you, Scott. Please tell me that Todd is at Steph's place, and I have you to myself."

"Yep, but only for tonight. We must leave tomorrow morning. Todd will pick me up, and you can say goodbye when he arrives."

Amanda watched as Scott spoke. There was something off about the way he spoke without looking at her. Giving herself a mental shrug, she decided not to borrow trouble. He would tell her the problem, but for now, he was hers. She ran her hand up Scott's chest and undid the buttons. He groaned as her fingers brushed across his bare skin. Scott fisted his fingers through her hair and pulled gently, angling her mouth for better access. His kiss was bruising and urgent, and Amanda responded to the invasion of his tongue by flicking her tongue against his. She wrapped her arms around his chest, and she massaged the muscles of his back. His hand cupped the globes of her butt, and she moaned as he pulled her against the firm ridge in his jeans.

"If we don't find a bed, I will do you on the table, Mandy."

"I don't care. Please don't stop."

Scott turned her around and pushed her up against the table. He divested her of her jeans and knickers, and the cold steel of the table pressed against her butt. When he pulled off her t-shirt and stepped into the gap between her legs, she felt as though she'd died and gone to heaven.

Eventually, they moved to her bedroom. As the night progressed, Scott's lovemaking became gentler and sweeter. This time together had to hold them over for half a year, and she had never seen him so tender and loving. While he wasn't a selfish lover, their times together were often passionate and sometimes frantic. When sleep claimed them, it was with his body wrapped around hers.

As Amanda prepared breakfast the following day, she tried to keep the conversation light. There was no need to discuss their impending separation; it had all been said the previous night.

"What time is Todd picking you up?" she asked.

Scott looked at the clock. "In an hour. We don't want to be late if we have traffic hold-ups." Amanda twisted her hands together, and her response to his pronouncement was a shaky "Sure."

Scott and Amanda sat outside on the patio, and the situation was surreal. They were chatting as though the most significant impediment to their relationship would not happen. When tears welled, she stood and moved away from the table; she didn't intend to make Scott feel guilty for leaving her. Behind her, she heard the chair scrape as Scott stood. He placed his arm on her shoulder and turned her face into his chest. She gave a shuddering breath and said, "I'm okay. The enormity of what's happening overwhelms me sometimes."

The tooting of a horn outside announced Todd and Steph's arrival. Scott grabbed his bag and headed out. Amanda followed Scott and approached her brother.

"Steph, can you come inside, please?' Scott asked. Amanda watched them and wondered why he needed to talk to her sister privately. Todd got out of the car.

"Well, 'Manda, we're off again. I didn't think it would be so soon."

"God, Todd, I will miss you. Stay safe; I don't think I'd cope if something happened to you. I love you, big brother."

He wrapped his arms around her. "I love you, too. We'll stay safe and contact you when we can."

Steph came out of the house. Walking towards Todd, she replayed her conversation with Scott, which had only moments ago. She could understand that he wanted to protect Amanda if something happened to him, but making Steph his next of kin held pitfalls. If Scott were injured, Amanda wouldn't be able to visit him in the hospital if the staff there insisted on only the next of kin. What would happen if Scott died? Steph would receive his pension and any assets, and Amanda would be entitled to nothing.

Steph shook her head. When she reached Todd, she pursed her lips. "Is there a problem?" he asked. "It's something I must sort out with Scott later."

With a forced smile at her sister, she said, "Your turn."

Steph turned back to Todd. "Why do we have to keep saying goodbye to you guys? Do you realise how much we miss you?"

Todd wrapped Steph in his arms. "I understand, but sometimes we must take different paths as grown-ups. We'll be back occasionally, so there will be time later for us to be together."

Amanda entered the house, the butterflies in her tummy running rampant and a tension headache thumping in her forehead. She saw Scott, her man —six feet of honed muscle, his short blond hair topping a face as hard as granite.

"Mandy, give me a hug."

Amanda walked into his arms and revelled in the strength of his embrace. Scott sighed and said,

"Sweetheart, I have been thinking about this deployment. This time, it should be with minimum danger, but the next time, it might be dangerous. I've designated Steph as my next of kin because if something happens, I would rather she tell you, not an army bigwig."

Amanda held her breath and waited for what he had to say next. Watching him, she realised that whatever he said next would be upsetting. He had yet to make eye contact with her, and his square jaw was so hard it looked as hard as granite. He spoke gently. "I love you, Mandy."

She let out a large breath. With Scott's declaration, she breathed again. "I love you, too."

"You know the saying 'if you love her, let her go'?"

Amanda went rigid with fear; her stomach rolled, and her vision blurred. What was he telling her?

"Mandy, it's unfair to tie you to a bloke who will be absent for months. If I'm disabled, I don't want you to be obligated to stay with me. Worse still, it would be for you to become a widow at your age. By the time I finish with the army, you may be too old to have children; I can't do that to you. I must end our relationship until I finish my stint in the force. When I come out, we can reconnect if you're still single, and I'm single too. Until then, we're done. Mandy, I'm sorry, that's how it has to be."

The blood left Amanda's face, and her head swam. She swayed on her feet. There was a hollow in the pit of her stomach. Scott, the man she loved, was calling it quits. Her voice came out as a whisper. "Please, Scott, don't do this. I love you; I can wait."

"Sweetheart, if I'm thinking about you. I put myself and my team in danger. I need a clear mind, and you're clouding it. If it's meant to be, we will be together when my service finishes."

Amanda watched Scott walk out of the house and out of her life. The pain that engulfed her brought her to her knees. She let out a low keening sound and collapsed onto the floor.

Outside, Steph watched as Scott walked towards the car. There was something wrong with the way he kept his head low and refused to look at her. He slid into the car and slammed the door.

"Let's go!" Scott said.

Todd looked sideways at his mate and then pulled away. Just before Todd pulled away, Steph glimpsed Scott's face. The tears in Scott's eyes froze Steph's blood, and for a moment, she stood stock-still. The conversation with Scott about next of kin resurfaced in her mind.

"Oh, God no," she murmured. With a chill in her heart, she raced for the house. Steph's heart thudded as she clattered up the stairs to the house's front door. She pulled up abruptly when she saw Amanda collapsed on the ground. "Dear God, no," Steph said as she lowered herself to the ground to comfort her sister. Amanda's face, ravaged with pain, looked pleadingly at Steph. "Why?"

As Steph shook her head, she held her sister and knew nothing would ever heal Amanda's hurt.

Epilogue

The house held an eerie silence, the essence of Todd and Scott still present in the rooms where they had lived. Amanda's distress was so great that Steph had called the family doctor, and the sedative he administered would keep her asleep and calm for most of the day. What happened after the sedative wore off was anyone's guess.

Steph mulled over the small amount of detail she had gleaned from her almost hysterical sister. Something about having kids and being disabled: none of it made any sense to Steph, and she sat trying to make logic out of the situation.

When the phone rang, she was tempted to ignore it, but she finally picked it up. The deep voice on the other end was instantly recognisable.

"Steph, I've only got a minute, but Scott told me what he said to Amanda. How is she?"

"How do you think she is? She is heartbroken. I had to call the doctor, and he sedated her. She's a complete mess."

A string of profanities was the reply.

"God damn, he had second thoughts about his relationship with Amanda after the announcement about our deployment. We discussed what could happen while we were here, and I thought he had overcome his fears. He thinks he's being fair to her, and I can't convince him that there is no kindness in breaking someone's heart."

"I don't know the full story; Amanda was too incoherent for me to decipher what happened. You can tell Scott I'm so angry that he'd better keep to himself for a while."

"I've gotta go, but if it's any consolation, he is distressed and second-guessing his decision."

"Todd, it's no consolation. I hope his heart hurts as much as Amanda's."

"Look after her, Steph. No recriminations, okay?"

"I understand that. Accusations and the laying of blame won't help Amanda now. Scott may be able to put this behind him and move on, but it will stay with her forever. When he finishes with the army, Amanda will still be single, not because she's waiting for him, but because she won't let anyone get this close again. You'd better go. I love you. Stay safe, big brother."

"I love you, too. I'll do my best to stay safe."

Also by Robyn C Rye

Farnsworth Sisters
Marrying a Rogue
Rescuing Hannah

The Buckingham Sisters
Lady Maggie's Challenge
Layla's Unwanted Husband

The Evans Family
Sometimes Love is not Enough
Still the One
Moving Forward

Standalone
One More Chance
Lady Jayne's Reputation
Third Time's the Charm
Can't Stop Loving You

The Marriage Scam
An Unlikely Match
Searching For You
The Unexpected Suitor
The Lady and the Duke
Starting Over
An Unforgettable Stranger
The Duke's Revenge
The Temporary Wife
Against The Odds
Betrayed
No Good Turn Goes Unpunished
Lady Eloise's Soldier
Lillian's Forbidden Beau
Remember Me
Always Second Best
When One Door Closes
Coming Home to You
Chasing Shadows
Fool Me Once
Deserting Lady Audrey
My Unlikely Saviour
Lies and Deception
A New Beginning
Julia's Second Chance
The Hidden Enemy
The Maiden's Redemption
Miss Elizabeth's Season

www.ingramcontent.com/pod-product-compliance
Lightning Source LLC
Chambersburg PA
CBHW022023150726

47990CB00002B/779